Jerry the Magpie

OTHER BOOKS
BY KINGSLEY ROSS HILL

The Further Adventures of Jerry the Magpie

Cave Days

Gower of the Hills

Nan's Nan and the Pirates of Port Eynon

Who was Taliath Saren

I'll meet you at Pennard Castle

Long Time a Ghost

Melody's Gift

The Mermaids of Mumbles Series, Oriel's Adventure

Jerry the Magpie

by
Kingsley Ross Hill

Published in Swansea Wales by King of the Castle Publishing.
ISBN 978-1-7778660-2-0 [Paperback]
ISBN 978-17778660-3-7 [E-Book]

To contact Kingsley Hill email gowerofthehills@gmail.com

Book design by Spica Book Design, Victoria, BC.
Printed and bound in Canada.

This book is dedicated to my great boyhood friend, Jerry the Magpie. Thank you, Old Boy, for flying into my life, and changing it forever! You made so many things right that had been so wrong.

To my brother Fraser Mark Hill. We don't choose our relatives, only out friends, but out of all the people in the world, I would have chosen you to be my brother, and you are! I love you dearly.

To my darling boy, "Boy Boy Doggy Dog," who I love more than words can say, and who has crossed the swelling tide before me. I long to see you again my friend. We will be together again one day. I know it! Please wait for me. I know you will.

About the Author

Kingsley Ross Hill was born near the city of Swansea, in Glamorganshire, South Wales and grew up in the village of Pennard, on the Gower Peninsula. [The word Pennard, means "village without a gate" in the Welsh language]. Kingsley, describes growing up in Pennard, and on the Gower Peninsula, as "living the most wonderful adventure, with no fences or gates."

It is interesting that the Gower Peninsular Series, which includes the books, *Cave Days, Gower of The Hills, Nans Nan and the Pirates of Port Eynon, Who was Taliath*

Saren, I'll meet you at Pennard Castle, and *Long Time a Ghost*, all give the reader, such a sense of freedom and adventure, like walking through a land without gates or fences. The authors books are full of humour, mystery and adventure, and are extremely accurate in their portrayal of the history and geography of the Gower Peninsula itself.

Kingsley is humble about his many achievements. He is becoming well known in his native Wales, and throughout the United Kingdom, and more recently in Canada and the United States, for his unique style of writing.

Kingsley lives with his family in the Creston Valley of the Rocky Mountains of British Columbia. He is also a pastor and counselor and has a youth outreach ministry.

Kingsley is an ex-pupil of Gowerton Grammar School, in Gowerton South Wales, and is developing into one of the most outstanding writers of his generation.

Table of Contents

JERRY THE MAGPIE
A Poem

The sun spoke golden over Norton Woods, and the dancing shadows fled to their hiding places.

The fields and hedgerows lit up and sang back to the morning's gay song. Even the haunted castle was now friendly, the ghosts had all gone.

The rooks in the rookery cawed, drowning out the quieter dawn song that was sung while the fields were still silver, all silver night long.

And inside I felt my soul shout, it's a brand new morning!

Then flash, black white, black white, I watched him dance with the golden morning. Up down, up down, bobbing over the hedgerows and flying with the dawn. Could it be my magpie? Could Jerry have been reborn!

Always you live, Jerry, always you live. I have told my children how you flew into my life like a song. You made so many things right that had been so wrong. Oh, Jerry, I still sing our happy songs! And on the day you died, I cried, and said, one day I will write, and tell the whole world the story of our song. A love of a boy and his magpie. Listen to our song.

Chapter One

A Day I Had Been Waiting For

The morning was full of spring's gay song! Its sweet scent hung heavy in the morning air, and it was as if my soul recognized this new morning, as a day I had been waiting for. Yet, what had I been waiting for? I listened carefully to the song that was being sung around me and was told of a story that started today.

Reaching the post-office in Park Mill village, I turned the old brass doorknob. It was locked! "The post-office isn't open on Sunday's," said a woman walking her dog, or was the dog walking her? I took a closer look. "You will have to call back tomorrow, it's open then, but if you want to mail a letter, there is a post box just down the road in the stonewall on the corner," she called back, as the dog continued to drag her with his leash.

"Thank you," I shouted. "I'll call back another day!" People are friendly in the village as well as most dogs. As I walked along the village road, I grieved the loss of not being able to buy a Mars Bar, and ten Refreshers if you please. I rolled my fifty pence piece in my fingers and wondered why they hadn't made the edges round like they had on the other coins? And I wondered if the Shepherd's Store would be open; it was just opposite my older friend Joseph's house.

I arrived at the Shepherd's Store, and it was closed too so I crossed the road and walked over the narrow stone bridge that led to Joseph's house and Park Mill Woods. As I crossed the bridge, I saw several large trout in the river, and I thought that if I lived in Joseph's house, I'd go fishing everyday!

I knocked on the door, and Joseph answered. "Come in," he said excitedly! "I've just got to put on my shoes and coat and we can go. Let's walk through the woods to the valley," he said, closing the door behind us. "Have you ever walked through Park Mill Woods, Kingsley?"

"Yes, a few times," I replied, "but I usually go to the valley from Pennard golf course, close to where I live. It's only a half hour walk from my house."

As Joseph and I walked through the woods, he pointed out several bird's nests along the way. We were both keen on collecting bird's eggs, along with half the other boys in our neighbourhoods. Joseph showed me a woodpecker's nest in a hollow tree, along with a little owl's nest in a rotting stump of a pine. We peaked in at the baby owls with their round heads and big staring eyes. They looked warm and snug, huddled together in their soft down coats. "They nest there every year, Kings," Joseph said, "and I've got one of their eggs." We also found a jay's nest and observed both the male and female birds carrying twigs and wool to line the nest with. I began to think about the magpie's nest that Joseph was taking me to see.

"The magpie is a member of the crow family," he said. Being shy, I held my tongue, but I probably knew as much as he did about birds, and maybe more. My Dad had taught me a lot about all the different birds, not only the species on the Gower Peninsula, but all over England and Wales. "The biggest member of the crow family is the raven," Joseph continued. "And the smallest is the jackdaw. There is also the carrion crow, and they are really bad pests! The farmers hate them because they peck the eyes out of the new born lambs in the spring."

"That's horrible!" I protested. "I'd like to shoot one."

"And then there is the hooded crow, with the grey neck and head. They are quite handsome looking but are a real predator too."

"I've never seen one of those," I said.

"No, there aren't any around here," Joseph replied. "You must go up to Carmarthenshire in mid Wales to see one. They get them in parts of England too."

The more we talked about birds, the more excited I got about seeing a magpie's nest. "You can tame a magpie, and even teach one to talk," Joseph said. "You can tame crows too, but they aren't as nice as having a magpie. My older brother had a magpie and tamed it! And he had it for about five years, until he moved away to England to work."

"What happened to it?" I asked.

"Oh, he sold it to the man in the pet store, and do you know what was funny?"

"No, what?"

"Well the man used to swear a lot, and he didn't know that my brother had taught the magpie to talk. One day when the man opened the pet store and said good morning to the magpie, the magpie said, 'shut up and make me a cup of tea, and if I had a face like yours I'd teach my arse to talk!' Joseph and I roared with laughter!

"I wish I had a magpie," I said. "I'd like it to tell Mrs. Bridges, who lives up the street, to 'shut up you fat cow'," and we laughed some more.

We walked along the riverside now, as the Park Mill river becomes the Three Cliff's river at the beginning of the valley.

"Where does the Park Mill river start?" I asked.

"It starts underground, somewhere on Fairwood Common, and travels underground until it reaches Ilston Village. And from there it travels down Ilston Combs, until it reaches the old Park Mill School. And after running through Park Mill Woods, it becomes the Three Cliff's River. It's a river that has three names. Four really, but the fourth name is a secret! One day I'll tell you, Kingsley, if you turn out to be a good friend." I didn't answer, I just thought about what Joseph had said. I think I'll make a good friend, I pondered. I like Joseph. He likes a lot of the same things I like doing, like catching trout and collecting bird's eggs. He's not very athletic though and doesn't like playing football like me. But that doesn't matter, I don't play football every day, and I don't have many friends. When you're beaten up and bullied, it affects your self-esteem and you feel unworthy of friendship. You don't believe that anyone could like you back. At least that's how I felt, like I had to earn or buy friendship. I couldn't just go out and make a friend. What if they find out what Kingsley Hill is really like, and how screwed up my life is?

As Park Mill Woods opens into the Three Cliff's Valley, the footpath steers away from the river into open grassland, and then a marsh area, and then you walk closer to the river again further down the valley. We arrived at a thicket of Hawthorn trees, and Joseph pointed out a messy bundle of sticks, high up in one of the trees. "That's a magpie's nest," he said, "and is the only bird's nest with a roof on it. Magpie's are very clever, because they build a roof over their nests! Often, they will use the same nesting site for many years, and you can see the layers of different nests underneath the roof." At first the bundle of sticks in a hawthorn tree seemed a bit of a let down, as I'd imagined something far more spectacular in my mind along the way. "It's all very quiet now," Joseph said, "but you just wait! The magpie's are probably out finding food for their young in the nest, so let's sit still so we don't scare them away and we will soon see the parent birds arriving back with food." We sat down in the thicket and waited expectantly.

It seemed like ages, then, suddenly, the previously still and quiet hawthorn trees became full of movement and noise and the sound of cackling magpies filled the valley air. "I told you they would come," Joseph whispered with a big smile.

"Yes, you were right! This is so exciting, I've never seen magpie's feeding their young before."

"Something's wrong," Joseph said. "One of the magpie's is swooping down to the ground. Do you see that?"

"Yes, I see it. And look! I can see a black and white bird sitting on the ground beneath the tree that has the nest in it. Can you see it, Joseph?"

"Yes, Kings, I can see it. One of the babies has fallen out of the nest. Let's wait until the parent birds fly off to get more food, and then we can go and investigate. If we go now the magpie's might attack us. They can be quite aggressive when it comes to protecting their young."

We waited until the adult birds flew off, to find more food. "Follow me, Kings," Joseph said and I followed him deep into the thicket of trees. As we got close to the tree I could see that it was a baby magpie that had fallen out of its nest. Its black and white feathers were shiny and glistened in the late morning sun, and there were still areas of soft down between the feathers, as my little friend sat still on the ground with its bright sparkling eyes fixed upon me. Had it been expecting me to come and rescue it, I pondered? I hoped so.

"If we handle it, we will have to keep it, Kings!" Joseph said. "Once a parent bird smells a human scent on the young, they will abandon them, and they will die." That didn't sound right to me. What bird could abandon its own babies? But I wasn't going to argue, I wanted to keep it as my pet.

"Can I keep it, Joseph?"

"Yes, you can, but you must promise to look after it. Here," he said, picking it up from the ground and putting it in my arms. It was all so exciting, I thought, as I unzipped my jacket and felt its little warm body against my chest.

"What should I feed it?" I asked.

"They like garden worms to eat, and milk to drink. That will give it the nourishment it needs, and give it water of course. Come on, I'll show you how to feed it some worms, that's what they are fed in the wild, as well as mice and frogs." Joseph lifted a few rocks on the ground and picked up some worms. "Now bring the bird out from your jacket and hold it tightly in case it gets scared. That's it, hold the wings tight against the body and hold it close to you, so that it feels secure." As I held it tightly, Joe lifted a worm to its beak. I could feel its body trembling and it wouldn't open its mouth to feed.

"It's not eating," I said, adjusting my grip so I wasn't holding it quite so tightly. Suddenly the bird flinched its feathers and wRidgleyled, so I held it more tightly again.

"No, it's not going to eat now," Joe said, dangling the juicy worm in front of the beak one more time. "It's alright," Joe reassured me, "it will eat when it's hungry. It is probably too scared right now."

Before we left the valley, Joseph climbed up the hawthorn tree to have a look at the chicks that were still in the nest. "There are still four chicks in the nest," he shouted down and then quickly climbed down before the parent birds came back. "If they see me up the tree, they might dive bomb me, and then abandon the nest," he said.

As we walked back to Joe's house, through Park Mill Woods, I felt so excited about my magpie, and thought of a name for it.

"How do you know that it's not a girl?" Joe asked.

"I don't," I replied. "It just seems like a boy. And if he does turn out to be a girl, she'll have a boy's name, because I think I will call him Jerry. Jerry the magpie!"

"Jerry's a good name," Joe said. "I've got an uncle named Jerry."

When we arrived back at Joes' house, his mother was home, and she was not best pleased that we had brought back a magpie, and she insisted that we not have it in the house.

"I have had enough of magpies to last me a lifetime," she said. "We finally got rid of your brother's magpie, and you brought another one home!"

"It's not mine," Joe insisted, "it's Kingsley's! The magpie fell out of its nest, and I'm going to show Kingsley how to look after it."

"You make sure that's all you do, Joseph, and you make sure that you take that bird with you when you leave, Kingsley!"

"Yes Mrs. Brooks, I will."

As Joe sulked for a few minutes, embarrassed by his mothers words, I took comfort in knowing that Joe would not change his mind and keep the magpie for himself. He's mine, I celebrated. I've got a baby magpie!

Once Mrs. Brooks left the room, Joe began to relax again, and said, "okay let's take him out into the garden."

After we were outside, I unzipped my jacket and held him like I did before, holding his wings against his back and holding him close to my body. Joe got a shovel from the garden shed and soon dug up a handful of worms. Then he said, "watch this!" He squeezed the sides of Jerry's beak until it opened, and then fed him a worm.

"He gulped the whole thing down at once," I said excitedly!

"Now it's your turn," Joe said. "Hand him to me." So, I lifted him into Joe's arms, and he handed me the worms.

"Now the first thing you need to remember, Kings, is that the chick's beak is still soft, and if you squeeze it on its sides, the bird will open its mouth for you. It doesn't hurt it. It feels the pressure on the sides of its beak, and then it's like a reflex, and it will open its mouth for you to feed it, and once it feels the worm or bread, it will try and swallow it down whole."

I gently began to squeeze the sides of its beak, and it felt soft and rubbery, and sure enough, it opened its beak wide, and I fed him a large worm which he devoured whole. "He's even trying to swallow my finger," I laughed, and I fed him another worm. "Look," I said excitedly. "He's swallowing my finger again!"

"That is his swallowing reflex," Joe said proudly. "I told you it would be easy to feed him."

"You were right," I said smiling.

"And you can do the same with bread, Kings. You just dip it in warm milk, and he will eat it as readily as he did the worms."

"Thanks for showing me," I replied. "Now I know that I will be able to feed him when I get home." After feeding Jerry the last of the worms, I zipped him up in my jacket and he fell asleep.

As well as feeling excited, I felt a great responsibility to take care of this wonderful treasure that I felt warm and soft inside my jacket. I would try and be the best dad that I could be for him. Joe went on to tell me about some of the exciting things that his brother experienced with his magpie.

"When he's older, he will sit on your shoulder, and even fly around and come back and land on you!"

"I wonder if he'll ride on my bike with me," I said. "He can sit on my shoulders while I'm riding." It was all so exciting!

I spent most of the afternoon with Joe, and as I walked back through the village, I thought how nice it was to be called Kings, instead of Queensley, and Mental Case, and other wounding names that the bullies called me at school. Joe was called Pip for short, because he was small for his age, and I'm sure that he didn't like being teased either because of his size. At least he wasn't punched and kicked Monday to Friday like I was, and that's only the physical beatings I took. There were the mental and emotional ones too, but there wasn't anyone I could talk to about those it seemed. Anyway, today was a special day and I'd made another friend. I walked through the village as proud as punch, with the magpie in my jacket.

My thoughts now turned to how I was going to tell my parents that I had gotten a magpie. I already had enough animals to start a small zoo, including four ducks. I had a wild Mallard duck that just arrived one day in the pond and never went away. My father had also built an aviary where he kept over fifteen different budgies and finches, and a cockatiel, which was his most recent pride and joy along with his racing pigeons. He once had a steaming row with my mother, and only communicated with her via pigeon over a period of several weeks. Mother said he was a bad communicator, but I thought it was bloody marvelous! More people should communicate that way, just like they did in the Middle Ages. Mother soon changed her tune when my Dad sent her a gold ring attached to one of the pigeon's legs. It was his way of saying sorry, I think, and it worked!

My Dad tried training a falcon once but it knocked one of his prize pigeons out of the air, and then ate it in one of our neighbour's gardens. Mrs. Tucker said we were a family of cannibals, as she watched in horror from her living room window as the falcon left her a bundle of guts and feathers to clean up. My father then tried to explain that it was only the falcon that ate family members, and that the rest of us hated the taste of one other!

If I proved I could take care of the magpie my father wouldn't have a problem in allowing me to keep it for a pet. Mother however, would present more of a challenge and would probably resort to naming all the other creatures I have had as pets over the last several years, and not looked after them according to her strict behavioral attire, which apparently, I didn't wear very well. She would no doubt bring up the squirrels that I kept in the top drawer of my dresser, and the hedgehog that I'd kept in the bottom drawer, which crapped all over my underwear and socks. Oh, and she hadn't been too impressed about my snake, which was still missing somewhere in the house, after frightening several of her friends that came over for her coffee hour last week.

I would have to give mother a real sob story, about how Jerry had fallen out of his nest, and was all alone in the world. He was a magpie too, and magpies are a wild bird that can fly around and do their own thing, and then come back at night and sleep in the aviary with the budgies. 'He won't bother anyone, mom. In fact, you won't even know he's around!' I think I've rehearsed my lines quite well, don't you think, dear reader? Yeah, but you don't know my mother. She can smell a rat a mile away.

It was early evening when I arrived home, at number 73 Browns Drive. Jerry was still snuggled and warm inside my jacket. As I peered through the living room window I saw my father sitting in his sacred leather chair, or as mother called it, his throne. My mother and brother were sitting on the couch.

I opened the door and walked straight up the stairs to my bedroom. Running up the stairs would only draw more attention to myself.

"Hello, Kings," my father shouted out.

"I'll be right down Dad, I just need to get changed." I pulled my socks and underpants out of my top drawer and stuffed them into the lower drawer of my dresser. Jerry was sleeping as I gently lifted him out of the warmth of my jacket, to his new home in the top drawer of my dresser. "There you are, Jerry Boy, you can have the penthouse suite." The challenge would be keeping my mother out of the bedroom for as long as I could, at least until I broke the news to her about having a magpie. It was a good thing my Grandparents weren't over this weekend, otherwise I'd have them preaching to me. I can just hear them now, saying, Kingsley, you've got enough animals around, without bringing home a magpie! He's a wild bird, and you can't keep a wild bird in captivity. I tend to agree with that, but when a bird falls out of its nest and the parent birds don't take care of it, then that changes things, doesn't it! I'm keeping him and that's that!

After tucking Jerry in with a heap of socks around him, I gently closed the drawer and went downstairs to join my family in the living room.

"Why didn't you come straight in and say hello?" my mother asked. I think she could smell a rat already! She always had this keen sense of knowing when I was up to something.

"Oh, I just wanted to go upstairs and use the bathroom first," I replied. "How are you, mum, did you have a good day?"

"Good day, my arse, he's up to something," my Dad announced from his throne. My brother laughed at my father's words and knew something was going down. It was 6:00, and Batman was on television, and I never missed that show by going upstairs for ten minutes. Jumping Jack Batman, what's going on with Kingsley? I don't know Robin, you will have to ask the Joker!

My brother kept quiet until after supper, and then pressed me as to what was going on. My brother Fraser was as stubborn as a mule, and if he thought he was missing out on something cool, he wouldn't stop hounding you until you revealed your secret.

"So, Kings, what's going on?"

"Nothing," I replied. "Why do you think there's something going on?"

"I know you, Kings," he said with a twinkle in his eye.

"Okay, Fraser, I'll tell you. But you must keep it quiet and not tell mum or dad, otherwise it will ruin everything!"

"What is it, Kings! What is it?!" he repeated excitedly. "What have you got, I won't tell anyone, I promise!"

"Okay, come in and close the door, and we have to pretend that we are playing a game so mum and dad won't suspect anything."

"Okay, Kings, let's put out the chessboard, and we can pretend we are playing a game of chess."

"Good idea," I said, "but we have to keep an ear out for one of them coming up the stairs." My brother was a good partner in crime when we were in cahoots together, but a deadly opponent when on the opposite side. He had the chessboard set up in no time and had all the pieces set up like we were in the middle of a game. "That's great Fraser, now you can go and look in the top drawer of my dresser."

"What is it?" he mumbled to himself, as he slowly opened the drawer. "Bloody Nora, Kings! Is it an owl or a hawk?"

"No, it's a magpie! He fell out of his nest, and if we had left him he would have starved to death. So, I'm looking after him, and I'm going to tame him."

"Wow, that's great, Kings! Can I hold him?"

"Yes, alright, as long as you're really careful. Hold him with both hands and keep him close to your body so that he can feel your warmth. That way he will feel secure and not be afraid."

"Wow, he's great, Kings. He's going to be the best pet around. I hope that you will share him with me. I can help find him food and feed him."

"Thanks Fraser, I'm really going to need your help. Especially keeping him a secret for as long as we can, you know what mums like, she will want me to put him back in the wild. If he goes back in the wild, he will die, it's as simple as that."

"I'll help you, Kings, don't worry. What do you feed him?"

"Garden worms and milk are his staple diet. In the wild he would also be fed mice, amphibians and insects. And of course, he needs water too."

I sent Fraser downstairs to get some bread and milk, so we could feed Jerry the way Joseph had showed me with the worms.

"Now you hold him, Fraser," I said, lifting Jerry into his arms. "That's it, hold him tightly but don't squeeze him. Make sure you hold his wings down against his body and hold him close to you so that he feels secure, and I will feed him."

"I can feel him trying to move, Kings, like he wants to get away."

"That's because he is nervous and doesn't know you yet," I replied. "Just keep holding him and he will settle down." I dipped a piece of bread into the milk until it was nice and soft and then squeezed the sides of Jerry's beak with my other hand, just like Joseph had taught me when we had fed him the worms. Jerry opened his mouth widely and gobbled down the bread.

"Wow! Look at him eat, Kings! He's not going to starve, are you boy!" I fed him six more pieces of bread dipped in the milk and he gobbled them all down. "What about some worms?" Fraser asked.

"Oh, the bread and milk should be enough for now," I replied. "We will go and dig some worms for him in the morning."

After Jerry had finished his feed, I tucked him back in the top drawer of my dresser, surrounded by my socks and underpants. "I'd love to see mum's face when she discovers Jerry in your top drawer, Kings," Fraser said, beginning to laugh.

"Don't remind me," I replied. "She hasn't got over the squirrels yet!"

Fraser and I played a few games of chess, and then went back downstairs, so mum and dad wouldn't get suspicious. I was sure glad that it was Sunday tomorrow, as that would give me time to come up with a plan as to where I was going to keep Jerry long term. It would also give me time to get a supply of garden worms to last me the week while I was at school. It was only early April, and it was still dark quite early in the evenings, which didn't give me much time to do anything after finishing my homework.

My biggest concern was keeping Jerry quiet during the day while I was at school. He seemed to stay quiet in my dresser drawer, which was working for now. If only I knew what day mum was going to do the laundry this week, then I could put him somewhere else for that day. My Grandmother was a lot more predictable. She did the laundry on the same day and time every week. She even went for walks to the post-office and visited friends at certain times during the week, and my brother and I could get up to a shit load of shenanigans! I would have to take my chances with mum however, and hope that Jerry would go undiscovered until next weekend, and then I would have to break the news to her and dad that I've got a magpie.

My first few days of having Jerry at home were exciting! I couldn't wait to get home from school and spend time with him, as I daydreamed the long hours away. 'You're not concentrating on your schoolwork, Kingsley,' all the teachers said. Though that was nothing new. There were only four things I looked forward to at school. Morning and afternoon breaks, lunch time, and the end of school bell, which rang at a quarter to four. Oh, yes, and each morning, I got to see Lorna Griffiths and her long smooth legs. Her lovely eyes were as blue as the sky, and I felt nervous every time I was near her. Once I got to sit behind her for a whole week! Her long flowing hair reached all the way to her bum, and I dreamed of getting lost in her hair and smelling her perfumed neck. Who cares if I couldn't see the blackboard! Twice or thrice in the middle of class, Mr. Richards, the teacher, asked me what I was thinking about. I couldn't tell him that I was thinking about the mysteries of Lorna Griffiths, so I made something up quickly! "I'm thinking about why you call the blackboard, black, when it's green?" I said. And everyone laughed. But in Mr. Richards eyes, I could see that he knew what I was thinking about, or very close to it, so he moved me to a seat at the back of the class. Oh well, at least I could still see Lorna's hair and her painted toes underneath her chair. And when the class windows were open, her perfume was carried on the breeze to meet my nostrils at the back of the class.

"What are you thinking about now, Kingsley Hill?"
"The blackboard is still green sir!"

Back to my magpie. Every day after school, my friends wanted to come home with me and see Jerry. Even people who weren't my friends pretended to like me, so they could come and see him. It was nice to be so popular for once, even if they didn't really like me and only wanted to see Jerry, my self-esteem was reaching an all time high. It usually operated in the high minus, so this felt good.

With a steady stream of "new friends" following me home after school, and coming into my bedroom, my mother began to wonder what the heck was going on. My reason for playing soldiers, and trading football cards was wearing thin. Mum could smell a rat! Or should I say a magpie? But she hadn't found him yet!

My usual dream of eloping with Lorna Griffiths to some tropical island had been interrupted last night, by a dream of one of my mother's friends breaking the news to her at the ladies coffee hour, that I had a magpie!

Time was short, before she would find out, that was sure. And when I arrived home from school on Friday, she was waiting to pounce with the solemn news that she had found my magpie! 'Wild bird', she called him, 'and in the top drawer of my dresser, in my underpants and socks!'

"I didn't say anything, Kings," my brother Fraser assured me, as we came through the door with a crowd of about six other kids following behind us.

"You must all go home," mother announced, closing the door behind them, and then turning her attention back to me. "Have you no respect for your mother at all? I thought you had learned your lesson after the squirrels, Kingsley, and that pole cat! And that's not to mention the pigeons and the owl you kept in the cupboard for a week. They almost stunk the house out! This house is not a zoo. What do you have to say for yourself?"

"He fell out of his nest mom! What did you expect me to do, leave him to die? I saved his life mum! I'm being kind to animals just like you and dad have always taught me. What's so wrong with that?"

"Nice reply, Kings," my brother said, just by the expression on his face.

"That's not the point, Kingsley! After the mess the pigeons made, you promised me that you wouldn't bring home any more animals without talking to your father and I first."

"Yes, and what would you have said, mum? Take him back to his nest to die!"

"Anyway, Kingsley, I knew that you were hiding something from me. All these children are following you home after school! Half of them you don't even like."

"I know, mum, they just wanted to see my magpie. But it was nice to be popular for once you know, instead of being the class dunce, who must go to Mrs. Morgan's 'stupid class', because I can't learn!"

"You can learn, and you're not stupid! You're one of the brightest fourteen year old's in the whole school! You can memorize five hundred different football players and tell everything about their history and careers! And, the only reason you must go to Mrs. Morgan's class is because you have asthma, and you have missed so much school. It's not a 'stupid class'. It's for pupils who need some extra help to get caught up!"

"Yeah, you try telling that to my regular class mates! They laugh and call me stupid, everyday! And you're right! The only reason half those other kids came home with me, and pretended to be my friend, was because of my magpie, mum! Do you know how that really feels? To try and deceive myself into believing that other people like me for who I am and not to see me as the 'stupid boy' with asthma, who's never at school, and even when he is, he's at the bottom of the class, because he's too far behind to catch up! Do you know how that feels, mum? It makes me feel like there is something wrong with me! Like I'm not as good as everyone else!"

"Kingsley, you are as bright as they come! And I know that God has chosen you for something special in this life! You are gentle and kind, and you have a special capacity to love. You have been given wisdom beyond your years, and an ability to sense and understand things that most other people can't. You wait and see! God will turn all this around and make it a blessing in your life. He is equipping you for the very special plan he has for you!"

"Yes, yes, mum, you always bring God into it, don't you? Well, to be perfectly honest I don't care about him or his stupid plan! If what I have had to go through in my life is part of his plan, then I don't want anything to do with him."

"It is sad that you think about God like that, Kingsley, and as far as your magpie is concerned, you can talk to your father when he gets home from work, and if he agrees that you can keep him in the aviary, you can keep him. As long as he doesn't come inside the house."

"Did you hear that, Kings? Mom said you can keep your magpie if he stays outside!"

"Yeah, I heard it, Fraser, that's great, but I still must persuade Dad."

"I have an idea, Kings. I know how you can make Dad agree to you keeping Jerry."

"What's your idea?"

"Dad took his van to work today. Why don't you wash his car, and then ask him if you can keep your magpie? You know how much he appreciates it when one of us washes his car."

"That's a great idea, I'll do it."

Fraser gave me a hand washing my father's car, and I agreed to let him hold Jerry anytime he wanted. We soon had the car washed, and I waited in my bedroom for my father to get home from work. Dad has a good size aviary in the backyard, with a large bird shed, and flying area. It would be the perfect place for Jerry to live. Dad had nine breeding budgies, and several rare finches. But his favourite is Cocky, the cockatiel, who sits on his shoulder while he walks around the garden. He's even taught it to speak. When I was in the shed the other day, looking at my father's model airplanes that were hanging from the ceiling, Cocky asked me if I was going fishing! 'No, I replied, are you?' He then said, 'shut up, shut up, you silly arse', and I roared with laughter!

Dad finally arrived home from work, and I wondered why he was so often late? He's probably having a Joe's Ice-cream I thought. He noticed right away that his car had been washed.

"Who cleaned my car?" he said excitedly.

"I did, Dad," I said, with a smile growing on my face, as I responded to the happy tone in his voice. "And Fraser helped me."

"So, what's brought this on, boys? Whose window have you broken now? I've usually got to give you fifty pence each, or a king size Mars Bar before you wash my car."

"I want to talk to you about your aviary, Dad."

"Why what's happened? None of the birds have got out, have they?"

"No, Dad, nothing like that. I found a bird that fell out of his nest, and I need somewhere to keep him."

"What sort of bird is it?" he asked, as the tone in his voice changed.

"A baby magpie."

"A magpie! That's a big bird, Kings! I don't know if he would get on with the other birds once he gets older. Magpies don't take kindly to other birds, Kings. They kill them in the wild."

"He's just a baby, Dad, and I wouldn't have him roaming free with the other birds. I just need somewhere to keep him, while I'm at school, and where he can sleep at night. I want to tame him."

"Tame him! It might be more difficult than you think to tame a wild magpie."

"Please Dad, please! I promise to take good care of him, and I'll clean out the aviary for you for free. You don't have to pay me for a month."

"Well, ok, Kings. But if he gets aggressive as he grows, you will have to get rid of him."

"Ok, Dad, I promise! And thanks, Dad, so much!"

"And one other thing, Kings. You need to keep him in one of the smaller cages, even when he's in the bird shed. You can use the empty blue cage that I used for transporting the racing pigeons."

"Thanks, that will be great."

Well, I could keep my magpie, and it was Friday night with the weekend ahead of me. What more could I want? Maybe a kiss from Lorna Griffiths!

Fraser and I spent the evening digging for worms in the garden.

"What are you digging so many worms for?" Mrs. Harris, our next-door neighbour asked, peering out from her upstairs window.

"We are going fishing, Mrs. Harris," I said. She would find out about Jerry, quick enough. Most of the houses where we lived on Browns drive are semi-detached, so everyone knows everyone else's business most of the time. It's nice when you want company and friendship, but it's a real challenge, when you're trying to keep something secret.

We had about a hundred worms by the time we were finished, a good supply of food for Jerry. That would last him for a few weeks, I figured. I was wrong on that one. They lasted all of one week. Jerry loved his worms, and 'it was a sign that he was healthy,' my friend Joseph Brooks said.

After we had finished digging worms, Fraser and I went over to Downes Farm, to pick up some hay to make Jerry a bed with. Mr. Downes sold us a whole bale for only 50 pence, if we promised not to steal any. We made Jerry a nice little bed and got him settled for the night.

I worked every Saturday morning delivering milk and eggs around the neighbourhood, with a man called Philip James, who owned a delivery van and had a contract to deliver the produce from the farm. It was a fun job delivering milk door to door from Philip's truck, and I got to work with my best friend, Elwyn, or Eli as he was known in the neighbourhood. Eli had been my best friend since I was five years old, when my family first moved to Browns Drive. Eli was a great partner in crime, and Philip James, the owner of the milk round, is El's older brother. It was through my friendship with Eli that I got my job. My job earned me 7 pounds a month, which was good money for a fourteen year old in the 1970's.

After my milk round on Saturday, I spent the rest of the weekend bonding with Jerry. I took him for a bike ride, safely buttoned up inside my denim jacket. And on Sunday I even took him trout fishing with me in Park Mill River. The worms that Fraser and I dug, sure came in handy. Every time I put a worm on my hook, Jerry would open his mouth and make a squeaking noise, as if to say, give me a worm too! Which I did, and it became a routine. I started a new saying. 'A worm on the hook, means a worm in the magpie's mouth.'

The weekend was soon gone, and on Monday morning, it was back to school. Time sure does fly when you're having fun, and especially when you have a pet magpie. I fed Jerry six worms and gave him several pieces of soft bread soaked in milk for breakfast.

"Well, it is off to school for me. See you when I get home, Jerry Boy." Fraser and I walked to school as we did most mornings. Only this morning, I had a spring in my step, like I usually had after school on Friday's. I had a baby magpie, and everything seemed good in my world!

Chapter Two

The Toads

Two weeks had gone by, and Jerry was starting to lose his fluffy down coat. His new black feathers glistened with hues of greens and blues. "You look shiny and new, old boy," I said, rubbing his back and chest gently with my finger. When I tickled him under his beak, he made this low-pitched squeaking noise, as if my touch gave him comfort and security. I believed that it did, because this was the only time that he made that noise and snuggled up to my hand. My mind flashed to the schoolyard for a minute, as I thought of how Lorna Griffiths rubbed my back and hugged me each time after the bullies had punched and beaten me up. If only she knew how much I loved her. I'm just too shy to tell her. Maybe she can feel it, when I hold her tightly back. "I think she does, Jerry, I think she does. Just like you can feel that I love you."

Jerry made a louder noise when I fed him his worms and would try and swallow my finger. I was getting quite attached to my magpie already. I can understand such affection for a dog or a cat, people would say, but how can someone want a magpie for a pet? At least with a dog, once it's trained, you can throw him a stick and he'll bring it back, and a cat will curl up on your lap. But what does a magpie do apart from pooping on your shoe? I was about to find out.

The spring evenings were getting lighter now when I got home from school. And I had visions of Jerry, sitting on my shoulders, and riding on the handlebars of my bike as I played with my friends.

My two closest friends, Eli James and Bryce Morris who were younger than me, and of course my brother Fraser, decided to go on a bike ride to Fairwood Common. We decided to meet at Bryce's house, after Eli and I had finished our milk round on Saturday morning. Eli and I worked as fast as we could, and we had soon finished all our deliveries.

"This must be an all time record!" Eli's brother Philip announced, as we made our way back to the farm to unload the milk crates full of the empty bottles. "You boys must have something special planned, to have worked so hard and quickly today."

"Just going on a bike ride," we both answered.

After we had finished unloading the crates, we now came to my favourite part of my job. Philip would give Eli and I a bottle of milk to drink, any kind we wanted. We always chose the Jersey Gold Top milk, because it had all that lovely cream at the top of the bottle and it tasted so sweet. Sometimes I got to take a dozen brown eggs home for my mother, which I sold to her for a very reasonable price! I mean business is business, isn't it?

After drinking our milk, and with our pay in our pockets, Eli and I rode our bikes over to Bryce's house, where Olivia, Bryce's sister, opened the door and invited us in.

"Bryce and Fraser are upstairs waiting," she said. Olivia was all eyes and smiles when she saw me, and Eli said, "she sure fancy's you, Kings!"

"No, she doesn't," I said, pretending that I wasn't interested, but I fancied her too. Her deep brown eyes and blushing smile had made me feel like I was melting inside when she answered the door. Eli and I shouted up to Bryce and Fraser as we climbed the stairs.

"Come on, let's go!"

"There has been a change of plan. We are going to Broad Pool," Fraser announced, as we all stumbled back down the stairs.

"Broad Pool?!" Eli and I echoed back in disapproval. "I thought we were going to Fairwood Common, to hang out in the air raid shelters and find some more dirty magazines."

"No, let's go to Broad Pool," Bryce said. "There are toads there, and I want some for my pond."

"Sounds like a plan then," I said suddenly excited. "I'd like to get some toads for my ponds too. I've got seven frogs now, so I may as well get some toads as well."

Fraser laughed, and said, "more animals for your zoo, Kings?"

"Yeah, you could start a zoo," Bryce added. "How many animals do you have now?"

"I've got three racing pigeons that my dad gave me, three Muscovy ducks, and a mallard, four ponds with lots of fish in them, a tortoise and a hamster, plus two ferrets. Oh yeah, and twelve budgies and two parrots."

"The budgies and parrots are Dad's," Fraser piped out.

"Don't forget your snake and the polecat," Eli said laughing.

"Oh, Yeah, and I forgot the squirrels and my Barn Owl," I said, as everyone laughed.

"What about Jerry?" Fraser teased.

"Yeah, what about your magpie, Kings?" the rest of the boys echoed. "Can we bring him with us? He's the coolest pet of all!"

"Yeah, I'm sure he would like to come with us and check out some toads," I replied. "Let me ride home and get him while you dorks get ready."

Fraser and I rode our bikes home to pick up Jerry, and I zipped him inside my jacket. Fraser then asked my mother if we could borrow a bucket to put fish in.

"Fish!" she shouted. "Why do you want more fish? Don't you bring any fish home here boys. Do you hear me?"

"Yes mum," we said, heading for the door.

"I mean it, Kingsley! You have enough animals around here. And what are you doing with your magpie today?"

"He's coming with us Mum."

"That's good because I can't keep an eye on him today. I'm going out."

Before we rode away, I unzipped the top of my jacket so Jerry's head could stick out in the breeze. He looked like quite the cool dude, as we rode along on our bikes.

When we met up with the others, Bryce said, "he just needs some sunglasses, and Jerry would look like a real rocker."

"You're wearing your Elvis Presley jacket, Kings," Eli said. "I wonder if Jerry is going to be an Elvis fan too."

"I'm sure he will," I answered.

We rode fast down Link Side Drive, until we reached the top of Park Mill Hill. Park Mill Hill is one of the steepest in all the Gower Peninsula and so much fun to ride down on a bike. It is so steep that you have to push your bike practically all the way back up the hill, even if you are a strong fourteen year old.

As we weaved our way down the hill, taking turns to lead the way, the only sounds were the squeaking of our brakes and the shouts of excitement as each of us dared one another to go faster!

"Slow down you fool!" a woman shouted as Bryce almost separated her and her dog. I think we had all used half of our brake pads coming down the hill. As we reached the bottom, Fraser arrived first, and was naturally the hero, a title that he would retain, until the next time we raced down the foreboding hill.

As we crossed over Park Mill Bridge, we leaned our bikes against the wall and peered into the stream below to see if there were any trout. There were several nice ones there, and I vowed to come back and catch them another time. Bryce gave me a look which said, "if I don't get back here first and catch them." Maybe we could agree to a treaty, and come and catch them together? No, I'm not sharing those beautiful trout with anyone.

Once over the bridge, we were on the main Park Mill Road, which would eventually take us to Lunon Hill, which was another hill almost as steep as Park Mill Hill, only longer. We would have to push our bikes up there.

From Lunon Hill, we would get onto the main road to Cefn Bryn and Broad Pool. Cefn Bryn means 'Big Hill' in the Welsh language. As to how Broad Pool got its name, I don't know. It is not particularly long or broad, but rather an average size pond. But it is not without mystery and legend, as we will discuss more about later.

Half way along Park Mill Road is the Post Office and general store. Park Mill Post Office was our favourite sweet shop, because they sell football cards, which all my friends and I collected. And 'Refreshers', which are a long oblong shaped sweet that is chewy and lemon flavored. They are hard at first, and almost too big for your gob, if you try and ram them in at once. If you did, you dribbled with the flavour as your taste buds burst into life at the taste of the powdered sherbet in the middle. The four of us would sit on the bench outside the Post Office and 'dribbled like basset hounds', as an old lady often called us, as she was pulled along behind her dog which took her for a walk. I think that's the only time us boys were quiet, is when we had refreshers in our gobs, or when Lorna Griffiths or Heather Simpson walked past.

I think the woman's dog wanted a refresher, but there was no chance of that. 'You better stick with your bone,' we shouted out, as he continued to drag the old lady down the street.

My mouth is watering for a refresher as I am writing this, dear reader. Next to cold hard cash, football cards and refreshers were our standard currency of commerce and trade. Oh yes, and ginger beer, and dandelion and burdock pop were high on the list too, and occasionally a cherry cola, if the can was cold.

But back to today. We parked our bikes against the Post Office wall. My brother Fraser, complained bitterly, as he inspected his brake pads. "I only replaced these last week, and they are half gone. By the time we get back down Lunon hill, I won't have any bloody pads left!" We all laughed, until we inspected our own.

"Mine are worn to the metal, already," Eli complained.

"And they all smell burnt," I replied.

We now discussed what we were going to buy. Fraser had conveniently left his pocket money at home, and Bryce had just enough for two packs of football cards, which were five pence a pack. Each pack contains five cards and a stick of bubble gum. Both Eli and I had our 7 pound wages each, after being paid from our milk round. We were millionaires as far as Bryce and Fraser were concerned. Jobs were hard to get in the village, and I was fortunate to have one which

I enjoyed so much. The only other jobs were paper rounds which didn't pay much and required working in the early hours before school. There was of course babysitting, which was really for the girls. Us boys only babysat if the youngster we were supposed to be looking after had an older sister that we fancied. But one change of dirty nappies usually brought the real motivation for being there, into plain sight 'pretty stinking quickly'. This was the case with me, in my first babysitting experience. Gosh, the smell was terrible, and I didn't wipe her little bottom properly, according to her mother. As my friend Eli often said, 'if your motivations are wrong, you end up in shit one way or another!' Wise counsel for a thirteen year old, don't you think?

I checked on Jerry inside my jacket. He made his usual little squeaking noise as I rubbed his back to let him know that he was safe and secure after our mad dash down the hill.

"Can we have a look at him?" everyone asked. I unzipped my jacket and unwrapped him from my mother's dishcloth.

"That's mom's best dishcloth," my brother announced.

"Shit! It is too."

"Oh well, it will all come out in the wash," Bryce teased, followed by everyone else's laughter.

"That's not funny you, dorks!" I answered back. Actually, it was hilarious, but when I got home I'm sure the suds would fly.

As I held Jerry in my hands, everyone gathered around. "You must sit down to hold him," I insisted, like a protective mother. "Otherwise you might drop him. And stop crowding around, you're going to scare him." We threw a coin to see who would hold him first, and Bryce won the toss. As he held Jerry tightly, he commented on his adult feathers that were now coming through. There wasn't much down left now, and he would soon be getting his long tail feathers. The tail feathers were last to develop, and they helped with the bird's balance, my friend Joseph had said. Jerry now sat on my arm and pecked at the buttons on my shirt, while Fraser and our two friends went into the Post Office to buy refreshers and football cards. Pondering my wonderful pet that was sitting on my arm, had put me in a generous mood this morning, and I had given Fraser 20 pence to buy a packet of football cards and some refreshers for himself. I'd also given him another 30 pence to buy me two packets of cards, and whatever was left over to be spent on refreshers.

Eli, and I had the biggest and the best collection of football cards, more than any of the other boys who went to Pennard School. We had over three hundred different cards each. Eli is a Leeds United supporter, and I am Liverpool supporter, and Fraser is a Chelsea fan. Bryce couldn't care a monkey's testicles about football cards, as long as he had some refreshers to chew. He occasionally did buy a pack of cards though, knowing that if he got a Liverpool, Leeds, or Chelsea player, he could trade it for a profit to one of us. I once paid him two quid for three cards! Daylight robbery, my father called it, and said that Bryce would make a good businessman one day. We all learned to wheel and deal, and not too often to steal.

The other boys soon came out of the store, excited to open their packets of football cards. Jerry was quite amused by the bright wrapping paper on the refreshers and proceeded to walk about between us collecting all our wrappers.

"Magpies like collecting bright things," Eli commented, as Jerry tried to pull the silver paper off his bubble gum stick. Little did I know at the time, but Eli was speaking prophesy that day. Jerry's love for bright coloured objects, would lead to many of our future adventures together.

As we sat in the flavoured silence, chewing our refreshers, the quietness was only broken by the sound of our gob smacking and belching, which sometimes turned into a full scale belching competition, usually won by Fraser or Bryce. Eli and I focused on more sophisticated things like farting.

"You pack of pigs," a woman said, as she walked her dog past the Post Office, and then stopped for it to lift its leg to go pee. We all burped some more so we could live up to our new title of a pack of pigs. "I'm surprised you're not peeing in the street," the woman said with a scowl on her face.

"That can be arranged," Fraser said, standing up and pretending to undo his fly. The dog ended up pooping as well as going pee, and the old bat didn't even clean it up.

"I think we have come to a truce," I said as the woman pulled on the dog's leash and waddled down the street.

Jerry continued to make his rounds between us, seeing what else he could find. Every so often, he would ruffle his shiny new feathers, and then flap his short wings, as if he was dreaming about the day he would be able to fly. I thought of how exciting it was going to be when he learned to fly. I had visions of him flying free around the neighbourhood, and then coming home to me when he wanted to. We would have such wonderful adventures together, like cruising around on my bike, and going to the youth club and chatting up the girls. He will be a hero there too! But would he one day fly away and not come back? No, we are too close of friends for that! He will want to stay and hang out with me, because I'm the one who saved him when he fell out of his nest, and feeds and cares for him.

I will never forget the special connection we had the other day. When I was rubbing his chest gently with my finger, he pushed himself up against my hand and I felt his little heart beating. The years and memories of our days, I recognized, though yet unlived, and he looked into my eyes and made the softest squeaking noise that transcended any language barrier that I thought we might have between us. It was like a special understanding was born between us that day, right then and there in those few sacred moments. I didn't have to fully understand it. In fact if I did, it would make it somewhat less wonderful and mysterious.

There are times in our lives, when an event or an experience is something we know inside will always be a part of us. It is not seen with eyes, but rather recognized within our souls. We may only be fourteen years old but have the knowledge that we will remember and recognize this event or experience when we are forty. It will still be a part of us then, and we will carry it with us all our lives into eternity, because the soul never forgets and never dies. Later on in life I was to become a deep thinking preacher! Maybe this was my first sermon!

After eating our refreshers, and trading football cards, it was time to be on our way. Jerry had enjoyed his walk about and collecting our brightly coloured wrappers, and I had a new Liverpool Football card from Bryce. I'd outbid Eli by offering Bryce one extra refresher than he did, and I also gave him a shiny new five pence piece which clinched the deal. I think Bryce was becoming more like a magpie, being attracted to bright objects like shiny coins. Eli being a Leeds United fan anyway, didn't grieve the loss of the card too much, even though I was ahead of him now, in having more of a variation of players in my collection than he did. Eli did however have a better bird's egg collection than I did, but I was catching up fast.

I wrapped Jerry up in mothers dishcloth and zipped him back up in my jacket, and we were off to the races. Down Park Mill Road we sped, towards Lunon Hill.

The best way to tackle Lunon Hill is to approach it at speed, and peddle like heck as far up as you can until your muscles are burning!. Then you have to dismount, and push your bike the rest of the way up the hill.

Fraser led the way as the rest of us dabbled for second place, peddling like heck, and then resting our muscles again as we continued down the road like there was no tomorrow! Just before Shepherd's Shop is the turn off for Lunnon Hill. Fraser, still in the lead, took a wide turn taking his bike onto the other side of the road, just in front of some oncoming traffic. The rest of us slowed down screeching our brakes and prepared to make the turn on our side of the road. The oncoming cars beeped their horns in fear that we would meet them head on.

"Crazy!" a man shouted standing at the foot of the hill, watching us speed past him. We all managed to stay on our bikes as we took the corner, and peddled like heck up the hill. I kept going until the pain in my muscles was excruciating. I wanted second place! Bryce followed right behind me, and dismounted from his bike. Eli arrived laughing behind us, having said something to the old man as he passed him at the bottom of the hill. Once Eli had got off his bike, the three of us called out to Fraser to wait up as he was already a fair ways ahead of us up the hill. Fraser stood and watched while the rest of us hurried, pushing our bikes to catch him up.

"What took you?" Fraser teased, with a big smile as we finally caught him up.

"That was a blast!" we all said, but our muscles were as sore as heck.

"Gosh, the long hill is slow going when you're pushing a bike. This must be why they call them 'push bikes' instead of motorbikes," I said.

Finally, we reached the top and stopped for a few minutes to get our breath. We then got back onto our bikes and headed for the main road. The main road to Cefn Bryn and Broad Pool is still on a hill, but the climb is gradual so we were able to make it all the way to Broad Pool without getting off our bikes. As we got closer to the pool, there were dead toads all over the road that had been run over by cars. We could hear a high pitched ribbit-ribbit sound up ahead. I began to get more excited as I ran over the flat toads on the tarmac with my front tire, and the ribbit noise from the pond got louder. I pedaled as fast as I could now, reaching the pool first. I flung my bike down and raced down the small embankment to the water.

My gosh! I'd never seen so many toads in all my life! There were thousands of them swimming across the pool, and climbing up the banks, some were even stuck together!

"They're shagging!" Bryce laughed as he pulled a pair of toads apart and threw them in the bucket which he had carried on the back of his bike. It looked painful for the toads to be pulled apart by a big human hand.

"Don't touch them or you will have warts," Eli said, now arriving on the scene.

"Don't be stupid," Fraser replied. "That's an old wives tale." I then picked up two toads and pried them apart.

"These two were stuck together like glue!" I exclaimed. "They must be real porn stars!" Everyone laughed as we threw the toads into the bucket. As I watched them climbing over each other and trying to jump out of the bucket, I felt sorry for the two I had separated and dropped into the middle of what was now a frantic crowd. Would they ever find each other again? Would some other toad steal away their love, forcing them to shag someone else? For a few moments I wanted to turn the bucket upside down and allow them to find each other. What if Lorna Griffiths turned herself into a toad and I had to find her amongst this lot?

Suddenly, Bryce dropped about another 10 toads into the bucket. It was hopeless now, I thought. They would never find each other again! Fraser, now took on the job of guarding the bucket, and throwing the escapees back, as they jumped out trying to regain their freedom., and we all took turns being the prison guard.

When Fraser's turn came around again, he shouted, "we can't fit anymore prisoners in the bucket. They are escaping everywhere," he said, falling over with laughter. "We must have a hundred of them! We need to think fast."

"I know," I said, let's draw straws to see who takes his shirt off, and we can cover the bucket with a shirt." We all peered into the bucket at the dirty smelly toads, and then looked at each other. Reluctantly, we all agreed. One of us would give up our shirt to stop the 'great escape'.

Fraser picked four pieces of marsh grass, and it was time to draw straws! Whose shirt would never be clean again? The smell of toad, even if it was washed a hundred times, would never come off. Not me please, I quietly mumbled under my breath, as I drew the first piece of grass. Eli went next. Good, my blade of grass was longer than his, and Bryce's was even smaller. Fraser was last to pull. And this was the longest! Bryce had drawn the smallest blade of grass, so off came his clean shirt, never to smell the same again.

"Good morning madam," I said cheerfully as a woman walked by.

"I hope you're not taking toads," she said, looking knowingly at the bucket which now had Bryce's shirt tied over the top of it. "There may look like there are a lot of toads here boys, but did you know that this type of toad is getting quite rare?"

"No, madam," Eli answered, "we didn't." We all hoped she would walk away and not look into our bucket. And to our relief she left.

"Rare, my arse!" Bryce said. "Look, there's thousands of them."

"More like millions," Fraser continued. Anyway, we weren't letting the Nazi's escape, we all agreed on that.

"We've got enough," Fraser said. "We can't fit anymore of these stinkers!" And we all peeked under Bryce's shirt, and agreed, we had enough. I quickly checked on Jerry who was still fast asleep inside my jacket, and I wondered what he would have thought about all these four legged creatures?

We sat and discussed what we might do with our prisoners before heading back to Lunon Hill. The first part of our journey was fast and fun! It was almost all downhill, and we coasted our bikes, with our heads down into the wind, until we reached the top of the Hill.

Before we went down Lunnon Hill, Fraser checked on the toads, and I checked on Jerry. We were all present and accounted for.

"Let's blast!" I shouted. And off we went, too fast, screeching our brakes and doing skids on our way down. Cars and tractors often came up the hill, taking up most of the narrow road. And it was a matter of which one of us was the most brave or stupid! We dabbled and raced for the lead, speeding faster and faster down the hill! Fortunately, there was no tractor, cattle or sheep on the road, just a small car that pulled over, its driver shouting and beeping his horn as we raced by.

"Slow down you idiots," he shouted, and Eli put two fingers up as we raced past the Fuhrer.

At the bottom of the hill, you must make a sharp left turn at slow speed, and keep close to the hedgerow, otherwise you will shoot out into the middle of the road. As the corner came into view, we all screamed our brakes to take the corner, except for Bryce, who had worn out his brake pads completely and was forced to take the corner wide He shot out into the middle of the road, narrowly missing an oncoming car! The driver beeped his horn and called us idiots again, but before Bryce could come to a stop, he separated a woman and her dog, his front wheel riding over the dog's leash!

"Stop you fools!" she shouted. "I'm going to call the police!" The four of us roared with laughter, as we peddled like heck, up Park Mill Road towards the Post Office.

The four of us all rode in a row now, as there was no traffic behind us.

"That was a close one," we all said to Bryce, who was still shaking. Then suddenly we realized that it was the same woman and her dog who we had nearly run over coming down Park Mill Hill earlier.

"It was her," Fraser assured us, "with the red hat and the poodle. She will call the police for sure." And we didn't stop pedaling until we reached the Post Office. There we stopped to get our breath and wondered if the old lady would really call the police. The last person any of us wanted to see was 'Die Book and Pencil' the village policeman, who was getting to know us boys quite well.

"Let's get off the main road," Fraser said, "and we can rest on Park Mill bridge before climbing up the hill." We arrived at the bridge and rested again.

"I'm not carrying the bucket up the hill," Bryce protested. "One of you will have to take it." So, Fraser and I took turns passing the bucket back and forth, as we pushed our bikes up the hill. Eli looked back over his shoulders every hundred yards or so to make sure that we weren't being followed.

As we pushed and puffed our way up the hill, our conversation went back to what we were going to do with the toads.

"I only want three," I said, "to put with my frogs in my ponds. And I will have to smuggle them into the garden, as my mum has had enough of me bringing home animals."

"And I only want five for my pond," Bryce said.

"I don't want any," replied Eli. "If my old girl sees those toads, I won't be allowed in the house." We all laughed at Eli's words.

Then Fraser said, "don't look at me! We will just have to get rid of the rest and let them go!"

"We can't just let them go," I protested. "We need to have some fun with them."

"Yeah, Kings is right," Bryce said, "we cycled for miles to get them, so we need to have some fun getting rid of them." Then I had a great idea!

"The Staffords are away on holiday, and they aren't coming back until late tonight. I know because my mom is friends with Mrs. Stafford, and she's been feeding their cat."

"So," everyone said, "what's your idea?"

"Well, let's mail the Staffords some toads through their letter box. And when they get home tonight, they will have a rather surprising welcome. An invasion of toads in their house!"

"Shit Kings, that's crazy, I love it," said Eli.

"Yeah, I don't like the Staffords," Bryce continued. "Daniel Stafford is a real wanker!"

"And so is his brother Adrian," I added. Fraser didn't say anything, as we all looked at him to reply. He didn't have to. A big grin was written all over his face. So, we were all in agreement of my great idea!

"But who was going to mail the toads?" we all asked looking into one another's faces.

"Not me! Not me!" we all said in turn. There was a loud silence, for what seemed like a long time, as we all thought of the consequences of being found out.

"It's always the one who does the deed who takes the wrap," Eli reminded us, "and the rest of us will get off pretty easy." It seemed my great idea was sinking fast. Then suddenly my brother Fraser offered a reward that neither Eli, nor I could resist.

"Whoever mails **20** toads through the Staffords letterbox, gets to choose any **20** football cards from my collection, minus my Chelsea players of course. I'm not trading any of them." Eli was first to accept the deal, but then he thought more about sharing the blame if he got caught.

"I'll tell you what, Kings! How about we mail 10 toads a piece to the Staffords, and then we can both pick out 10 cards each from Fraser's collection?" That was good enough for me, I thought! And Bryce, who didn't collect football cards, made us shake hands to seal the deal.

"You bring out your whole card collection, not just the ones you want to get rid of." Eli insisted to Fraser.

"That's fine," Fraser replied, "but I'm not handing out any cards until there's 20 toads put through the letter-box, and I'm going to be right there counting, to make sure you put in 10 toads each! Bryce, you keep an eye out for the Staffords car, because they are due home this evening and we don't know what time."

It was decided after the toads had been mailed, we would all watch for the Staffords return from the spare bedroom window at our house which looked out right across to the Stafford house.

When we arrived back at Browns Drive, our dastardly deed had all been planned to the last croaking detail.

"I think the toads are looking forward to it too. Don't you? I mean at least they get to leap around someone's house instead of being stuck in a bucket!"

Fraser laughed at my words, and said, "I can't wait to see Mrs. Staffords face when a toad answers the front door!"

When we arrived at our house, mum was out, as she said she would be, and my father wasn't home either. That was a bonus, I thought we'd have at least one of them to contend with.

We parked the bikes in our back yard and carried the toads across the road to the Staffords house, which all seemed quiet.

"We will ring the doorbell first," I said, "pretending to call on Daniel or Adrian," neither of whom any of us liked. It was just a good excuse to ring the doorbell and make sure no one was home.

"They do have a dog though," Bryce reminded us.

"I'm pretty sure they took the dog with them," I added.

"What about Mrs. Bridges?" Fraser asked. "That nasty cow doesn't miss anything!" Bryce walked past her house to make sure she wasn't watching us from her living room window, which she often did on Saturdays when us boys were playing football in the road. She would often sit on a stool with her front door already slightly open, ready to waddle out quickly into her garden and grab our football when it came over her wall.

"I bet she has at least 10 of our footballs," I said, "including my best leather one that I got for my birthday."

"I remember that day well," Eli said. "You were so upset about her stealing your best leather football that you ran home to get another football, and placed it in the middle of her lawn and took a penalty kick right through her living room window! That will save her from coming out, you said, and we all ran up the street before she called the police."

"Yeah, I'll never forget that," I laughed. "That is what I call vengeance for all the soccer balls that the cow stole from us."

Bryce now returned with the news that old Bridges was gardening in her back garden and wouldn't see us.

"Wait a moment," I said. "My old girl knows that we were going to Broad Pool to get fish and she might put two and two together and come up with four. It will be obvious that we did it!"

I was hesitating now as I remembered my punishment for kicking my football through old Mrs. Bridges window. I had to stay in my room after school for a month, and even help put in the new window. And mailing the Stafford's toads wasn't going to fetch a lesser punishment if we got caught.

Fraser, now seeing the hesitation written on my face, upped the stakes. "I'll give you 20 cards each," he said. "That's 40 cards out of my collection."

"20 cards each!" I echoed back. "Let's go!" I know it was mad, but 20 cards each was worth getting caught for, and who knows, maybe we would get away with it. We crossed to the other side of Browns Drive, like the Magnificent Seven, only there were only four of us.

"The fab four," Bryce said.

"That's the Beatles, you idiots," Fraser replied, "and I much prefer Black Sabbath. I'm not Paul fRidgleyin McCartney," he continued, "now get a move on before the Stafford's come back and spoil the fun."

Three of us stood at the Staffords front door, like nervous ninja turtles, while Bryce stayed out in the road to keep an eye out for their car. Who was going to be Leonardo, and ring the doorbell?

"Well, here goes. Keep an eye out for the car," I shouted back to Bryce, and I rang the bell.

We waited for about two minutes, and there was no answer. Not even the dog barking. They had obviously taken him with them. They had a cat though.

"That should give old whiskers some fun, chasing toads," Fraser added, his voice now excited again as the deal was going through. "Get going with those toads," he said, "before they come home."

Eli untied Bryce's shirt from around the bucket, and the croak and smell of toad was horrid!

"They will need their carpets cleaned after this," I said, as I suddenly remembered my mum saying that Mrs. Stafford had just had her carpets cleaned last week. The word 'punishment' began to walk through the pages of my mind. Oh well, it was too late to turn back now. Fraser looked at Eli and I and began to hum the song, 'it's too late, it's too late now'.

"Shut up!" I replied, as the reality of what we were doing sank in.

Eli and I began pushing the toads one at a time through the letterbox. They croaked and twisted their legs as we pushed them through. We could see the rather obscure images of falling toads inside the house, through the frosted glass window at the bottom of the door. Frasers face beamed as he counted with delight, as one after the other found themselves to be new members of the Staffords household.

"Ok, that's 9 each," Fraser announced. "Come on, one more toad each."

Just as I was stuffing my last toad through the letterbox Bryce shouted, "Car! Car! There's a car coming up the road." We bolted like rabbits back across the road to our house.

"The bucket! The flipping bucket! You idiots, you have left the bucket!" Bryce shouted and Eli quickly ran back and got it. We put it in my father's shed and then raced upstairs to the spare bedroom to watch the action from the window. The car that Bryce had seen was one of the other neighbours, and had already turned into a driveway. Bryce continued to watch from the window, while Fraser brought out his football card collection. He threw a dice to see who had the first pick. Eli got the highest score, so he got to pick first. Scurvy luck! I wanted to pick first! Fortunately, he picked Gordon Banks, who I already had. I picked Ian Rush, of Liverpool, which was a rare card! For the next several minutes, I forgot about the good tidings of toads we brought to the Staffords, and I picked out 4 more Liverpool players, which completed my whole Liverpool team collection. Until the Staffords got home, I was a happy man! Eli was happy too, as he had picked out Johnny Giles and Norman Hunter, which almost completed his Leeds United collection. Fraser wore a brief look of regret on his face as we picked out the prize cards from his collection, but he was soon smiling again as he thought about the toads and the look that would be on the Staffords faces when they walked through their door.

Eventually the both dreaded and exciting announcement came. "There's a car coming, and I think it's them." I quickly stopped sorting my cards and swallowed nervously.

I looked across at Eli, and said, "you don't look worried."

"I'm not," he said. "I'm not even here. I've got an alibi. I'm going to cut a deal with my sister Debbie to vouch for me being with her all day today, if I babysit her puppy while she goes out with her boyfriend tonight."

"And I'm not here either," Bryce said. "I went over to my cousin's farm today, at High Pennard."

"I don't know what you pillocks are talking about." Fraser replied. "I haven't seen any of you lot in a week. I went fishing today with the Tucker boys."

"And don't look at me," I said, "I've been out with my magpie all day, and I don't know anything about any toads."

"Glad we got that out of the way," Fraser said. "I hope you guys have got a good memory, in case Die Book and Pencil interrogates us." Die Book and Pencil often visited us boys to make sure we were behaving but could smell a rat when we were up to something. "Now he will be smelling a different type of rat," Fraser laughed. "One that croaks and goes rippit-rippit."

As the Staffords car pulled into their driveway, we all watched from the window.

"You guys look like the Memphis Mafia," Fraser said. "Guilty as heck!"

I managed to put on a laugh, and then said, "put on the music and open the window, you idiots, or it will be obvious we are up to something!"

Mrs. Stafford opened the front door, then suddenly came running out screaming.

"Frogs, frogs! There are frogs in the house!"

Daniel and Adrian immediately went in to take a look, and Mr. Stafford tried to console his wife outside the front door, before going inside to investigate.

"Turn the stereo down," Fraser demanded, "I want to hear this." Soon we could hear shouts coming out from the house, as the front door remained open.

"Shit! What have we done?" I spoke aloud. "We were only having a bit of fun."

"I better get going," Bryce said, his face flushed and worried.

"Me too," said Eli. "Can we use the back door to the field?" Eli, just lived three houses up the road and could double back to his house from the field without getting seen, and Bryce could cut across the field and through Downes Farm to where he lived on Fox Hole Drive. Fraser and I raced to my bedroom, which was at the back of our house, and watched Bryce and Eli climb over the hedge, and into the field. Fortunately, as luck would have it, my mum was still out while the shenanigans were going on.

"What about the bikes?" I said to Fraser. "It's obvious that Bryce and Eli have been here! The first thing mum is going to see when she walks up the driveway is the bikes at the side of the house." At my words Fraser quickly moved the bikes from the side of the house to the back shed.

I decided to throw the bucket with the rest of the toads that was still in the shed over the hedge into the back field, before mum or dad arrived home.

"The last thing we need is for them to find the evidence of the bucket of toads," I said. Fraser watched with amusement as I slung the bucket of flying toads over the hedge. He then suggested that he and I take our bikes for a ride up and down our road and act like we know nothing about what was going on at the Staffords.

"That way we can feel things out, Kings."

"Yeah, you're right," I said. "Let's just act normal, like nothing has happened."

"What are you talking about," Fraser replied. "Nothing has happened."

But my conscience argued with my brother's words, and I said, "let's hope they don't call the police, because if they do, Die Book and Pencil will be around to talk to mum. And she knows very well that we went to Broad Pool, where there are toads."

"Shut up, Kings, and keep riding."

After riding around Browns Drive for about twenty minutes, we stopped outside the Staffords house to talk to Daniel and Adrian, who were standing outside their front drive.

"Someone has put toads in our house," Daniel said. "We just came home from a holiday at our Grandmother's, to a house full of toads!"

"Toads!" I echoed back, feeling as guilty as a Black Sheep. Maybe that's because the Hill Brothers, along with Eli James, were known as the 'black sheep' of Browns Drive. I managed to disguise my guilt, however, with my surprised tone of voice. "What do you mean toads?" I said aloud.

"You know what toads are!" Adrian Stafford, said angrily. "Someone has been in our house, and left toads!"

Shit! Now they think someone has broken into their house, I thought. This could become a more serious investigation! Fraser, now winked at me, and the expression on his face said, shut up, and don't say anything more, Kings, or you're going to sound guilty next time you open your mouth! And he was quite right. I did feel guilty, guilty as heck!

"Did you see anything while we were away?" Daniel asked, "considering you live right across the road from us."

"No, nothing," Fraser said. "We've been out on our bikes all day, so we haven't been around."

Now another neighbor, Mrs.Cowper, arrived on the scene. She lived several houses up the road from the Staffords. Mrs. Stafford must have called her to tell her the news, I thought. We called Mrs. Cowper, 'The Irish Cow' because she was from Ireland and looked uncommonly like a cow, and moo-ed at her husband several times a week. I used to be friends with her son Shawn, until he beat me up for singing a song about his alcoholic father, making fun of him.

In later years, Shawn would leave home and join the navy. If he ever came back, I would have to sing him that song by the Village People, In the Navy! In the Navy! Maybe not. Rather I will sing him a song with a two by four about the head. All considered though, Mrs. Cowper was a good Kerry Cow, and I felt sorry for her, as later on her husband would drink himself to death within a few years.

Mr. Stafford now reappeared out of his house, and said, to the Irish Cow, "there's no damage done, and nothing stolen, as far as we can see. All the windows are secure, so they must have put them in through the letterbox. It's damn kids, I'm sure of it. If I catch them, they will be sorry they were born!"

"You will, will you, Old Stuffy?" said Fraser under his breath. "The toads are to pay you back for all the things your son Daniel stole, including our bikes. Don't worry, Kings, they can't prove anything!"

"That's right Fraser, we were out all day on our bikes anyway. And what are they going to do? Fingerprint the toads? And what goes around, hops around, get it?" We both laughed.

"Yeah, the only worry now is Mum, Kings. We have just got to keep our story straight or she will smell a toad. We will just tell her that we were going to go to Broad Pool, but we changed our minds and went for a long bike ride up over Cefn Bryn, instead."

By the time Mum got home it was late, and nothing was said, other than, "did you boys have a good day?"

"Yes Mum, Fraser and I went for a nice bike ride to Cefn Bryn."

"I'm glad you boys had a good day and behaved yourselves," she replied. Maybe she forgot all about us going to the pond. We were safe, at least for now.

Chapter Three

The Unexpected Guest

The next day, Sunday, I spent the day with Jerry. After feeding him his garden worms and bread dipped in milk for breakfast, I sat him on my shoulder, where he stayed for almost the whole day. From time to time he would flap his wings for balance if I leaned too far forward or backwards, or knelt to look at my fish in the fishpond. I sat him on a rock while I fed my fish. He dipped his beak into the pond, and then lifted his head up again and began to drink. This was a little milestone in his life, because this was the start of him drinking on his own. I felt like a proud dad! Jerry also made runs back and forth across the lawn flapping his wings as I called his name. We did this several times and I think it was the Magpies equivalent of throwing a stick for a dog. I would pat the ground hard, several times with my palms, and call out, 'come on Jerry', and he would come skipping towards me. "You know your name, Old Boy, don't you," I said, and he would move his head from side to side, listening intently to my voice. "Here you go, here's a worm for you," and he washed it down with another gulp of pond water.

It's a great feeling to walk around with a wild magpie on your shoulder, and I walked up and down the road just to see what people would say. Every so often he would peck my ear gently and nibble on my hair, pulling at my curls. "Glad you like my hair, old boy, now stop it, it tickles." And I said, "I love you too." I'm sure it was his way of showing me his inquisitive affection, as we toured around the neighborhood.

In the afternoon, Mum went food shopping, and took my brother Fraser with her. Dad had gone up in his glider at the airport, which he did about every second Sunday, so I had the house to myself for a while. Mum had left some meat and a tomato for me to make a sandwich for lunch, but I fancied a cereal and made shreddies with hot milk and brown sugar. And I wasn't the only one who felt like some shreddies. After I'd taken a few bites, Jerry ran down my arm and sank his beak into my cereal. "Hey, you can't have my cereal, Old Boy! You have your worms and bread and milk to eat." But there was no stopping him, and he wolfed down one shreddie after another, and made what sounded like a very satisfied squeak each time he gulped one down. "Ok, Old Boy, you can have that bowl. I'm not sharing the same bowl as you." So I heated up some more milk and poured myself another bowl of shreddies. "Now you've got yours and I've got mine. Now you stick to your own bowl!" A few times he ran across the table and tried to taste mine. "No," I said, and gave him a gentle tap on his beak. After about six attempts and my continued taps on his beak and a gentle push across the table to his bowl, Jerry seemed to get the message. He looked at me with a mischievous gleam in his eye, and then finished all his shreddies. "That's good, Old Boy, now I don't have to go and dig you worms tonight." There was just milk left now in his bowl, and he couldn't lift it up to his mouth to finish it like I could. So, he hopped onto the side of his bowl, and lowered his beak into the milk to finish it. I got up to get a drink of orange squash from the fridge, and clash bang, crash! Jerry had turned the bowl of milk over himself and onto the floor. "Oh no," I said, "look at the mess, there's milk all over the floor!" Jerry shook his head and made a kind of squeaky sneezing noise.

Just then I heard Mum's car in the driveway, so I grabbed Jerry, who was still wet with milk, and took him out to the shed. "You stay here," I said, locking him in his cage. "I've got to go and clean up your mess, otherwise Mum will know you have been in the house. Don't look at me like that," I said, as he gave me this pitiful look in his beady black eyes. "Look, you stay there, and I'll be right back."

I quickly raced back and washed our bowls in the sink as Mum and Fraser came through the door.

"My son is washing dishes? This is a first!" Mum said. "There must be something going on for you to be washing dishes."

"No, there's nothing going on Mum, just thought I would do the dishes for you." Fraser knew better, as he looked at me with a puzzled twinkle in his eye.

"Hey Kings, do you want to go for a bike ride to Bryce's house?"

"Yeah, sounds good, Fraser. I think I will bring Jerry with us. You should see Jerry Pie, he's sitting on my shoulders now! I'm going to see if he will ride on the handlebars of my bike."

Jerry was excited to be out of his cage again so soon, and he flapped his wings with excitement as I lifted him onto my shoulders. Immediately, he started to peck my ear gently, and then he tried reaching his beak as far as he could down my ear. "Stop it! Stop it! It tickles," I said, as I lifted him off my shoulders and put him onto the handlebars of my bike.

I started pedaling slowly. He seemed to be comfortable with the wind blowing through his feathers for the first few minutes until I hit an uneven piece of road with a bump. Suddenly he jumped and flapped his wings, leaving the handlebars and landing on my lap. I quickly grabbed him with my left hand and steered the bike with my right. I put him back on my shoulder and took off again slowly. I could feel his feet gripping onto my jacket as we picked up speed.

"He's doing good, Kings!" Fraser shouted across, as he kept the same pace as Jerry and me.

Whenever the road got bumpy he seemed to get spooked, and over the next few bumps, he made his way down from my shoulder to my arm, and then on to the security of my lap. This was slow going, so I zipped him inside my jacket, with his head sticking out in the wind, and Fraser and I raced the rest of the way to Bryce's house.

When we arrived, Bryce's sister, Olivia, answered the door as always, and when she saw Jerry with his head sticking out of my jacket, she asked if she could hold him. Fraser headed upstairs to see Bryce.

"How old is your magpie?" Olivia asked.

"Well, I've had him for almost a month now, and he was just a baby when he fell out of his nest."

"Can I hold him?" she asked again.

"Yes, but I think it's better if you sit down with him, because he can't fly yet and often startles."

"How about we sit in the back garden, then if he tries to fly, the lawn is nice and soft, rather than the concrete," Olivia said.

Olivia and I sat down on the lawn and passed Jerry, back and forth. This gave us time to talk. We had often looked at each other in passing and wanted to be able to talk without Bryce or my other friends being present. Olivia's mother brought us out a drink and some biscuits, and she also wanted to hold Jerry. He was becoming a real celebrity around here. After Olivia's mum went back into the house, I heard Bryce and Fraser calling for me. Olivia and I looked at each other, and said in silence, 'our time has been interrupted again, and they will soon be here.' I finally grew the courage and said to her what I had wanted to say for a long time.

"Olivia, could I see you tomorrow after school? And would you like to come for a walk with me to Pennard Castle?"

She smiled and said, "yes, if it's okay with my mum." As Bryce and Fraser arrived on the scene, Olivia said, "I'll go and ask mum right now." Just as Bryce, Fraser and I started leaving, Olivia shouted out from her window, "Yes, I can come after five thirty tomorrow, when I've finished my homework."

"See you tomorrow then," I shouted back.

"What are you and Olivia arranging?" Bryce asked.

"Oh, I'm going to show her Jerry's nest," I replied. I didn't want him or Fraser to know that I'd asked her to come for a walk to the Castle with me. That would put a cat among the pigeons for sure, although it was obvious how we felt about each other just by the way we tried to steal a look at each other when we were around other people.

Bryce shouted bye to his mum, and us boy's rode away on our bikes to Southgate Village, and then on to Pennard Stores, where we could buy some refreshments and hang out. Jerry sat snuggled inside my jacket with his head sticking out in the breeze, as we raced our bikes to the store. He felt like a little hot water bottle as I felt his warmth against my shirt.

Pennard Stores had only just started opening on Sunday's, the Sabbath breaking sinners! All the other shops were closed on Sunday's.

"That is a good thing," my grandparents often said. "It's good for shops to be closed on the Sabbath. It helps to keep Sunday set apart from the rest of the days of the week." Sundays were family days in our home. At least every second Sunday, my mother took Fraser and I to Linden Chapel, in Mumbles. My father never came to church, but he was always keen for my brother and I to go. After chapel, he would pick us up, and if we had been well behaved, he and mum would take us for a Joe's Ice-cream, the best ice-cream in the world! Even if you hadn't tasted all the rest, you knew Joe's was the best. Some things you just know.

After our Joe's ice-cream, mum and dad would take us for a long walk along Swansea Bay, and we would collect driftwood and shells and tell stories of sea monsters and the mysteries of the sea. Dad said that "last summer a rather large woman lost her bra and knickers while swimming in the sea. And the fat cow has been called a sea monster ever since." Fraser and I roared with laughter, but my mother told my father off, for describing such a monster.

We now arrived at Pennard Stores, and we leaned our bikes against the courtyard wall, and went inside. Not seeing our favourite sweets on the shelves, all three of us walked up to the counter and asked for ten refreshers each. Mrs. Ridgley, who ran the store, counted out fifteen.

"Sorry boys, that's all the refreshers I've got left. So you can have five each, and don't fight over them. And what's that in your jacket, Kingsley? A crow?"

"No, Mrs. Ridgley, this is Jerry, my magpie."

"Good Lord! Whatever next? Your poor mother! Now don't let him loose in the store, otherwise there won't be any more refreshers for any of you."

"Alright Mrs. Ridgley, I won't."

We paid for our refreshers and a bottle of pop to share. There were a few large stones on the village green, which we turned over to find some worms for Jerry. We found four worms which I fed to him as we sat at a picnic table in the store courtyard. Jerry wolfed down the worms as the three of us took turns feeding him. After he had finished the worms he amused himself by collecting the empty wrappers from the refreshers just like he had done yesterday at Park Mill Post Office. He was sure getting used to people now, as he climbed and fluttered up and down on each of us, pecking our clothes and ears. Bryce was quite amused as Jerry played with his shoe laces until they came undone. "Look! He just untied my shoelaces," and we all laughed.

Just then, Eli arrived on the scene. "Where have you dorks been? I have been looking everywhere for you! Thanks for inviting me," he said sarcastically. "I called in at all your houses, and you had already left for a bike ride."

"Sorry," we all replied.

After chewing down our refreshers, we talked and laughed about the toads we had mailed to the Staffords yesterday.

"They will never catch us, because they can't prove it," Fraser said confidently. But Bryce and I weren't convinced, and we discussed out loud what we would do and what punishments we anticipated receiving should we be found out. Eli was quiet as he listened intently. "Shut up!" Fraser said. "We are not going to get caught!" But in his voice, I could detect a rare nervousness, as if he was convincing himself that everything would be alright. Fraser in my view would make a great Lawyer. He would keep a cool head no matter what was going down. I can remember when he and I aimed some fireworks at a neighbour's house last Guy Fawkes night. The old 'battle axe' Mrs. Bridges called the police. There we were, fireworks still in our hands, and Fraser said to the police, 'prove it. I haven't done anything!' He was my hero that day. When they started questioning me, I looked guilty as heck, and spoke all nervous like.

"I know you did it," the constable said to me. "It's written all over your face. But your brother could sell sand to the Arabs and keep a straight face."

Well, it was now Sunday evening and time to head home. I put Jerry on the handlebars of my bike again, and rode away slowly. This time he stayed on the handlebars all the way home. He was growing stronger everyday, and his balance was getting better.

When Fraser and I arrived home, we were greeted by a rather 'uninvited guest' who was sitting having a cup of tea with my mother. It was Police Sergeant David Jones or Die Book and Pencil, as we called him. We always knew that seeing him meant the death of our evening and he was always writing notes in this notebook and refused to use anything but a pencil. We thought it was a creative name at the time. Great I thought, what did he want?

"Kingsley and Fraser," he said, "I'd like to talk to you about some toads."

"Toads!" I exclaimed, trying to swallow with the lump that had instantly arrived in my throat.

"Yes, toads! Now where the devil were you yesterday afternoon Kingsley?"

"I don't know anything about any toads. I was out with my magpie yesterday."

"Good God! He's got a magpie, Mrs Hill. It's more like a zoo every time I come here. Last month it was the pigeons and that bloody ferret! Now, Fraser, my boy! What do you say about toads being mailed to poor Mr. and Mrs. Stafford?"

"Firstly, the Staffords aren't poor," he replied, "and secondly, what toads?"

"I'll tell you what toad's boys! Eli James has already confessed his part in this amphibious crime, which makes you boys liars! Now I know that Bryce didn't mail any toads, he was your lookout man. You, Kingsley, and Eli James did the actual delivery. And you, Fraser, put them up to it by giving them football cards for doing it!. Does that sound about right, or shall we all go and spend the night at the police station? I will personally take you four boys to school tomorrow."

"No, no, Mr. Jones, Sir. Coming to think of it, I remember now. That does sound about right."

"I'm glad that you have decided to remember, boy! I can assure you it's better this way. Now this is what's going to happen. Mr. and Mrs. Stafford need the grass in their rather large back garden mowed, and the lawn in the front needs weeding. Next Saturday afternoon, and the next three Saturdays after that, you four boys are going to be cutting lawns and gardening for Mr. and Mrs. Stafford." Both Fraser and I looked at Mum in protest, but she kept quiet, apart from saying, 'you better listen to Sergeant Jones!'

Sergeant Jones, continued to announce our sentence, and said, "Mr. Stafford has decided not to press charges of mischief, on the condition all four of you toad catchers apologizes to him and Mrs. Stafford, and show up for gardening duties. Any 'no shows' by any one of you boys, will mean a mischief charge for all of you down at the police station! I think that's more than fair, Mrs. Hill, don't you?"

"Yes," Mum replied in agreement, "that's more than fair!"

"Oh, and I will be driving by Mr. Staffords house for the next four Saturday afternoons, and if you boys aren't pulling your weight, I will find some work for you to do at the police station. Is that clear Kingsley and Fraser?"

"Yes, Sergeant Jones, it is."

"Good, I will see you boys and your other two partners in crime, next Saturday. Oh, by the way Kingsley, I hope you got some very good football cards for all this trouble?"

"Yes, I did Sir. Ian St. John, and Roger Hunt!"

"You're a Liverpool fan, are you?"

"Yes, I am."

"Well make sure that you 'never walk alone then.' That's their song isn't it?"

"Yes, sir it is."

"Any more toads in people's letter boxes, and you will be 'walking alone,' down the hill and around the corner to the police station," and Sergeant Jones laughed all the way back to his car.

Mum was quiet, but her face said it all. There was no supper for the Hill Brothers, no TV, and an early night. As I climbed the stairs to my room, I thought, I've walked this lonely walk before. It's like being on the losing team having lost the FA Cup, having to walk the long walk up through the tunnel at Wembley Stadium, and through the crowd to the waiting politician or member of the Royal Family, to receive the losers medal. The walk of shame, the winning team called it, as Kevin Keegan lifted the FA Cup again for Liverpool! And as I looked at my newly acquired football cards in my room. I could hear the roar of the crowd, as Prince Charles pinned my winners medal on my shirt, and I took a bow. Yes, it had been a tough game, but it was worth it! I opened my bedroom window, and held the FA Cup up in front of all my friends and neighbors. Who's that staring at me from across the road? Shit! It's Mr. Stafford. Well, I hope he's happy with his loser's medal. That's what you get when you play for Manchester United.

Chapter Four

Shanty Town

Monday morning arrived, and after wolfing down two bowls of shreddies with hot milk and feeding Jerry, I left for school. Monday morning was always 'stupid class' with Mrs. Morgan. I never left her class feeling less 'stupid' than when I had arrived. Her way of trying to get our attention and to focus on our assignments was to remind us that we were behind the other children in our learning, otherwise we wouldn't have to come to her class. Being behind in our learning, however, was always translated by the other children in the regular classroom as us being stupid mental cases and unable to learn.

After Mrs. Morgan's class I joined the non stupid kids for English literature with Mrs. Basset, who we called a Basset Hound, only she had smaller ears. I don't think I ever saw that woman smile. Only when she was punishing us boys by hitting us over the knuckles with her wooden ruler, did I ever see her expression change. It was a half smile and half smirk, Bryce called it. I think she enjoyed hitting us boys with her ruler, or yard stick as she called it. I don't think she ever used her stick on the girls, only on Ten Ton Tessie, the poor fat girl in our class who had a thyroid problem and looked more like a saddle backed pig than a girl. A lot of us felt sorry for Tessie, and tried to be kind to her, but not Mrs. Basset, the sadistic cow! She was a master of punishment to whoever her daily victim was. I liked Fraser's version of describing her. He said she was a 'stiff-faced, sabbath breaking, athlete footed, fly infested, mad cow! And if I had a face like that, I'd teach my arse to talk!' I laughed and laughed when he first said that.

Fraser and I arrived at the school twenty minutes before the bell and kicked our football around as usual. Bryce and Eli soon arrived, and after a little debate about the toads, we all agreed that we'd got off lightly and the whole ordeal had been worth it! However, I'm sure our tune would change by next Saturday afternoon working for the Staffords. Oh well, 'One day at a time sweet Jesus' as Tammy Wynette sang on the radio.

The bell rang and off we went to our classrooms. Fraser, Bryce, and Eli went to the same class. I was a year older so I went to a different class. We all agreed to meet on our lunch break and play football. We could rarely trade football cards at school because the bullies that ran the playground would threaten us if we didn't give them some cards, usually our best ones.

One of the advantages of going to Stupid Class on Monday mornings was you very rarely had to think very hard. I mean you were stupid anyway and unable to learn, so why not live up to your reputation. It gave you time to wake up from the weekend and dream about the wonderful sound of the bell at 3:45 when you would once again walk the green green grass to home. The clock on Mrs. Morgan's wall was the slowest in the school I'm sure, and sometimes I wondered if she purposely turned it back. But it was better than doing math in Mr. Davies class with the rest of my classmates. I could count football cards, marbles, refreshers, and my pocket money, and the freckles on Lorna Griffth's legs, and that's all the math I needed to learn.

This morning Mrs. Morgan gave us a nice piece of drawing paper and a box of new crayons each and said we could draw something we did on the weekend. My thoughts quickly went to my non-stupid classmates slaving away with their math in Mr Davies class. Who's stupid now? I thought, as I smelled my new crayons in their box and pondered what I would draw. There are two things that I love the smell of. Opening a new box of crayons, and playdough. Gosh I could almost eat the stuff! Come to think of it, there were three things I loved the smell of. The other was Lorna Griffith's perfume. I could smell her lovely slender neck all day long!

I drew a picture of Jerry riding on the handlebars of my bike and then spent the next hour dreaming about Olivia Morris and going for a walk with her this evening to Pennard Castle. I will bring Jerry along too, I thought. He can ride on my bike to Olivia's house and then I'll sit him on my shoulders as we walk to the castle. The weather looks nice too, I thought, as I looked out of the window and drifted deeper and deeper into my daydream.

"Wake up Kingsley!" Mrs. Morgan said with a raised voice, which was unusual for her. "We have been going around the class, Kingsley, and sharing with each other what we have drawn, and it's your turn to tell us about your picture."

"Well, this is my bike, and this is my pet magpie Jerry, riding on the handlebars. On the weekend, Jerry and I went for a long bike ride up to Cefn Bryn."

Some of the kids laughed at the thought of me having a magpie for a pet, but it didn't bother me. I knew how special Jerry was, and all they had were boring dogs or cats, or younger siblings that peed the bed. Most of the children in Mrs. Morgan's class were from lower class families, and often could not read or write properly. As I looked around the table, I recognized five children from Sandy Lane, or Shanty Town as it was known locally. We were a middle-class family according to my parents and grandparents, and sometimes the classes didn't mix. Then there was the upper-class, my father told me, and they were generally wealthy, and real snobs with a 'I'm better than you attitude.' My friend Eli said that he knew a family from the upper class, and they wiped their asses with five pound notes. I'm happy with a fifty pence piece, thank you very much!

Some of the children in Stupid Class smelled like a rhinoceros, and wore ragged old clothes, including George Matthews, who sat next to me. The worst thing about George Matthews, apart from his stale smell, was his glass eye, which wept with yellow mucus. I learned very quickly to eat my sandwiches before class or while looking in the other direction. He could even take his glass eye out of his eye socket, leaving the rest of us boys and girls traumatized by the shocking sight of the red blood vessels and blue veins at the back of his head that played over and over in our minds like Count Dracula and the Body Snatchers. George was also in my regular school class, only I didn't sit next to him there, and if I did, all the other children would call me names and tease me about liking 'Cyclops', as they called him.

Anyone who lived in Shanty Town, or was friends with any of the lower-class children, was not accepted, or allowed to play with my middle-class peers in the playground. The Sandy Lane children were judged and despised for where they lived and their social status. Most of them lived in rundown shacks or gypsy caravans as my Dad called them. I was teased, ridiculed, and beaten by the bullies anyway, because I went to 'stupid class' and had asthma attacks and was always too far behind to catch up with my schoolwork. I think therefore I was able to relate to George Matthews and the other children who lived in Sandy Lane. None of us were accepted by the crowd. My perception of why I was rejected and bullied, differed from the opinions of my peers. I felt it was because I am gentle-spirited, sensitive and kind, but they perceived it as weakness and cowardice. This was especially hard for a boy growing up in rough and tough industrial South Wales. I played cricket and football, wrote poetry, and didn't fight or play rugby, only when I had to.

In many ways I experienced both worlds; the prejudice put upon the children of Shanty Town, and the privileges of being born into a middle-class family. One of the things that I learned early in my boyhood, was that most of the children from Sandy Lane were gentle and kind, and appreciated the little they had. I felt in some way drawn to them. Was it because I was never rejected by them, but rather accepted and esteemed in their presence? Their poverty and vulnerability seemed to give them a truth and a simplicity that I did not see amongst my middle-class peers. Or was it because I was able to see my own privilege through their eyes? Sometimes when I saw their poverty and walked with them for a few miles in their plight, I felt embarrassed, even ashamed for the wealth and plenty that I enjoyed.

Regardless of the eye and smell, George Matthews was a true friend, and the times I turned my back on him just so I wouldn't get beaten up because of my association with him, really bothered me! He would see the bullies coming towards us in the school yard. Sometimes he could even feel them coming before they were even in sight, and I wondered how he could do this? It was uncanny.

As the bullies came towards us, I could feel the dread of his heart as his eyes made contact with mine, and I could see so much more into the torment of his soul. He would say, 'Kingsley, you better get going, or they will beat you up too.' I would watch from afar, or in my hideout in the crowd as they mocked and beat him and called him names. Once the bullies were gone, I would go over and try to comfort him. Gosh, I wish I was brave enough to bleed with him! Sometimes his nose would be broken where they had punched him, and he'd cry and say, 'I wish I wasn't poor, Kingsley, I wish I was like you.' And for a few minutes I would feel sorry and ashamed, because I lived on Browns Drive, a nice middle-class housing estate, while he lived and bled because he was from Shanty Town. In one year, they broke his nose five times! The doctor said that the bone never had time to heal, and it always set crooked.

When my brother Fraser and I rode our bikes over to Shanty Town, the children there called us the 'rich kids', yet we were not rich, but very average in wealth, compared to the upper-class, my mother had told us. But I always felt rich! We owned a nice four bedroom, two storey modern house, and a holiday caravan in West Wales. My father had a cabin cruiser in the harbour. He owned two cars and four motorcycles, and each summer we went on lovely holidays around the country and went camping on long weekends and bank holidays.

I remember several times when I was beaten up by the bullies, punched and kicked. Everyone walked past me and laughed. Fraser, Bryce and Eli were in different classes and had other friends to hang out with besides me, so I was all alone at these times, except for George Matthews, who always came and sat with me after my beatings. He never turned his back on me like I did on him. He wasn't ashamed of what others would think or say. I think a part of it was he had nowhere else to go and certainly less to lose, but I knew he cared, and that made him a true friend to me.

Suddenly the school bell rang, waking me from my daydream, and we were dismissed from Stupid Class. As we headed out of the classroom into the hallway, George looked at me in the hope that I would spend some of the breaktime with him. Not today, my expression answered him back, I would have too much to lose. I had arranged to play football with Fraser, Bryce and Eli, and another five or six boys who would usually show up. We would then pick teams, and they did not like Cyclops playing with them. Why should they? He was from Shanty Town, stunk, and had a glass eye. As we finished picking teams, they shouted out at George, who stood and dreamed, and hoped of one day being allowed to play.

"Hey Cyclops, do you have to take out your eye to cry?" And as I kicked the ball around with my friends, I could feel his loneliness from afar, and I remembered how he had come to my side after the bullies had beaten me up just the other day. I pushed my thoughts aside and continued to play. He would understand, he always did, a picture of sadness off the grid. And besides, I couldn't hang out with him today. I was seeing Olivia this evening, and I didn't want her to see me with George Matthews.

After a good game of football, the bell rang for the end of our morning break, and I was off to regular class.

"How was stupid class,stupid?" some of the boys asked, as I found my seat and sat down. "Can you smell something?" they asked each other, having turned their attention to George. "Why don't you take your eye out and have a look around, Cyclops, you glass eyed twat!" He didn't answer, and to our relief, Mr. Davies, our teacher arrived, and class began.

"Today we are going to continue our study of American history," he said. Firstly, I felt relieved that we weren't doing math. I was so far behind in mathematics that there was no way I could catch up, so I had given up trying. Secondly, I felt a little excited, as history was one of the subjects I enjoyed and was good at. As well as art, and sports, and of course sitting near Lorna Griffiths, she was my favorite subject!

Today we learned about Lord Nelson and the defeat of Napoleon, and the time went by quickly. At least now it was lunch time, and today was bangers and beans, and roast potatoes, my favourite meal at Pennard School. The dining room was segregated into two areas, one for the girls who were served first, and then another area for us boys at the end tables closest to the teachers table, 'so that we would behave,' Mr. Davies often reminded us. I didn't need reminding, I thought, I just wanted to eat my meal without being teased and threatened.

Each table sat eight pupils, which included a server and a helper. The server was responsible to serve the correct portions to each person at the table, and the helper helped as necessary, including taking over the serving position if the server was away ill.

Next to break times in the school yard, sitting at the lunch table was the clearest way to see the prejudice and privilege expressed between the social classes. Personal prejudices also came into effect. If you were from Sandy Lane, you were given a smaller portion of food, and not allowed second helpings until the middle-class kids had been offered it first, except when one of the teachers came over to the table to see how things were going, then things were equal until he returned and sat down again at his table.

I was once denied a second helping of sausages and beans because of my friendship towards George Matthews. He sat next to me at a table for about six weeks and received significantly less food than the rest of us. Once, a server asked each person at the table what their father did for a living, knowing that George's father was unemployed, and we were given food portions according to the social status of our parental jobs and material possessions. Fortunately for George, the helper had fallen out with the server, and reported him to one of the teachers who promptly came over to our table, and served George an equal meal like the rest of us. Some servers were open to bribes for larger portions of food. The wheeling and dealing started right after the first break when we changed classrooms for our next subject. It usually took the next teacher a few extra minutes to get to the classroom, by which time we had made our deals. Jeff Adams was our table server, and each Monday I brought him a football card to trade for a second helping of my favourite food. He also accepted money if you were fortunate enough to have some. Money also bought you protection from the school yard bullies. I spent on average of twenty five pence a week, half my pocket money on protection. It was frightening to be punched or kicked in the head when you were twelve or thirteen years old. I was fourteen, and still too afraid to fight back.

Jeff Adams and his helper Mervin Howel brought our food to the table today as usual, and I ate my favorite food. Adams was in a generous mood today, and he served George Matthews a regular amount of food. The discussions at the boy's tables were almost always the same. George and I were not permitted to say anything at the table, unless Adams or Howel asked us something. So, we listened to the other boys discussing how the First Division Football Teams had done over the weekend, who had what football cards to trade, and who fancied what girls in the school. And then there was that dreaded discussion as to who was going to be beaten up after school. Today I was relieved to know that it would be the new boy who had just started our school last week who would take a beating, not George or me. Adams had asked the new boy for a packet of football cards, and the boy said no, they were his brother's cards, and he wasn't giving them away. So today after school Adams and a few of the other bullies were going to teach him a lesson. I had taken a beating two weeks ago because I didn't pay my twenty five pence for protection. George was beaten regularly because he never had any money or football cards to trade. The official announcement as to who was being beaten up was announced during the afternoon break, and by the time the end of school bell rang at 3:45, it seemed the whole school knew who the lucky person or persons were who would be set upon by the ruthless bullies of Pennard School. Half the school seemed to show up for the beatings, forming a circle around the event and then getting as close as possible to whoever it was who was getting beaten up. They formed a circle so that teachers and parents couldn't see. Getting into a punch up was one thing but being watched by half the school was even more demoralizing, and if you ever told any of the teachers who it was who beat you up, the bullies beat you up every day for a month, as I had found out! I had been so afraid of these thugs, that I had begged my mother and father not to go and talk to the teachers after I had arrived home with black eyes and bruises. But today I was 'popular' at the lunch table, because of Jerry, my magpie.

"I hear you have a magpie, Kingsley," Adams said. He usually called me 'Queensley'. "That is a great pet," he said. "I wish I had a magpie! I want to see him sometime, Kings, ok?"

"Yes, okay," I replied keenly. And I wished I could be Jeff Adams's friend. If I could be his friend, no one would ever lay a finger on me again, because Jeff Adams was the toughest, meanest boy in Pennard School.

"How about you bring your magpie to my house after school tomorrow," he said. There was silence at the table while Adams spoke, and George looked away. I wanted to enjoy the moment, but my gut instinct told me that Adams had another motive for asking me to bring Jerry over to his house. But hey! It was worth a try to try and win his approval, wasn't it? George's face, and everyone else's at the table told me otherwise, Anyway, it was arranged, I would take Jerry over to his house tomorrow after school.

After I finished my lunch, I met Fraser and Bryce on the soccer field, where we played until the bell rang for the last lesson. Last lesson on Monday was English Literature and Grammar. Gosh I hated it! I could read and write, wasn't that enough? Apparently not! I was so embarrassed last week when Mrs. Basset asked me to stand in front of the class and write a paragraph on the board. I misspelled two words in one sentence, and everybody laughed! And I hoped that this week, Mrs. Basset would remember that I couldn't spell and went to stupid class. Or would she ask me up to the blackboard again today, knowing that it would get a laugh from my peers?

As everyone else read and reviewed their English grammar textbook, I daydreamed about getting home to Jerry, and going for a walk with Olivia this evening. Finally, the last bell rang, and I walked home with Fraser. As we passed the green outside the school grounds, my classmates, and other pupils began to form a circle around the bullies and the new boy who had just started at our school.

"He's going to get his head kicked in," Fraser said. I just wanted to pass by as quickly as we could and head for home, in fear the bullies would turn on me. We managed to sneak past and made it home safely.

A Walk to the Castle

When we arrived home, Fraser and I went to check on Jerry.

"He is getting bigger," Fraser said, "and look how long his tail feathers are getting."

"It won't be long before he can fly," I replied, "maybe even this weekend." We dug Jerry some worms and fed him, and I also cleaned out Dad's aviary as I had promised I would. Fraser put Jerry on his shoulder and walked around the garden.

"He's the best pet anyone could have, Kings," he said. "He's awesome, and everyone at school will wish he was theirs!" Just then Mum called us in for tea. She had made hamburgers and chips, which was one of our favorites.

"How was your day at school?" she asked. Fraser mumbled something with his mouth full of chips, while I continued wolfing down my hamburger. After we had finished eating, Fraser went to do his homework, while I claimed I didn't have any. Always being so behind at class was no motivation for doing any anyway, and when I did, it usually came as a reminder of why I was in Stupid Class.

Every time we started a new school term, I would sit for a few minutes, hours if I could, and contemplate the blank piece of paper lying on my desk. It represented a 'new start'. The teacher would ask us to write our names and answer a few questions on the shining piece of white paper that illuminated upon the old wood-stained desk as if inviting each pupil to scribe out their own destiny with a pen or pencil. The smell of new books and the box of new crayons on each of our desks greeted my nostrils, evoking memories and caressing my senses, and filled the classroom with the aroma of new hope. For me though, my destiny seemed to have already been written out within the walls of Mrs. Morgan's asylum, and within a few weeks of the new term, the ghosts of my past failures returned to haunt me again, stealing away my secret hope and taking its virginity.

As the teacher wrote his class rules and expectations of us on the blackboard, it was during these few moments that I felt akin, and equal to my classmates. We all sat under the blackboard together. Our behaviour would be governed by the chalked rules written above us, as Mr. Davis stood like a King over his subjects with a ruler in his hand! No lessen had yet been taught and no homework given, and no stupid class had been attended. The bullies had not yet threatened and spoken their demands, and the school football team had not been picked. The blank piece of paper on my desk shouted out to me again! And I dreamed of being able to write my own script and change the narrative that stood before me like a cruel prison guard. Soon I would be taken to my cell of teasings and beatings, and the shame of going to Mrs. Morgan's class would strike again! Oh, how I wish I could lose all this pain.

As Fraser continued to do his homework up in his room, I sat on the couch in the living room. Fraser thought I was a hero, getting away without doing any homework, but my quiet thoughts haunted me. The words of my Psychiatrist Dr. McDonald seemed to be attacking my heart and mind.

"I'm sorry to have to tell you Mrs. Hill," he said to my mother, right in front of me. "Kingsley isn't like the other children. He has a learning block and can't learn. We have done the tests and he is unable to cognitively grasp the concept of what he needs to learn for his academic development, Mrs. Hill." Or translated into my language, he said, "stupid can't learn like the other children," and an inner voice was telling me that it was true! McDonald's words rang in my ears and permeated deep into my heart. My self-esteem had hit an all time low.

It is easy for other people to tell you who and what you are without understanding your unique makeup and struggles as a human being. I wondered if Dr. McDonald knew what it was like to have an asthma attack and be fighting for breath, and then having to be away from school for weeks and even a month at a time, recovering. Then you go back to school and you can't catch up. You are laughed at and mocked and told every day that you are stupid! How can you fight back and not believe it, when the enemies of doubt and fear surround you on every side, threatening to overwhelm you like the crashing sea!

Last July, my teacher Mr. Davies congratulated all my classmates on the last day of school for passing their year of studies, and he told them he was proud of them for having learned enough to graduate, and to be able to move up to the next class in September.

"I will miss you all," he said, "except for Kingsley Hill, who has missed too much school and needs to catch up. He will be staying here with me for another year." Oh, the shame and the pain that I felt inside, and he had said it in front of the whole class! I could hear my classmates whispering and snickering, 'stupid is having to stay behind for another year, I'm glad he's not coming up to the next class with us. They should keep him and Cyclops in Mrs. Morgan's class forever!"

And then there was the bullying. How can school be a place of learning, when everyday you must deal with pain and abuse, and just try to survive! Most breaktimes I had to run and hide from the thugs who stalked me. No, Dr. McDonald, you have no idea why I can't learn. Some days I just want to give up and die. I'd thought about jumping off the cliffs but I was too afraid that I might survive the fall and end up in a wheelchair. Sometimes I didn't go to school even when I was feeling alright. Why should I go to that war zone where all I learn is pain and rejection. My Grandfather said that If I didn't behave and change my ways, then I'd be going to hell.

"Hey Kingsley," Satan whispers, "look at your life! Nobody likes you, and you can't even spell. Why don't you kill yourself. Life is much better down here with me in hell. Why don't you do it? Come on, just give up! There is no future in this world for you!"

"Yes, there is! I've got a magpie and he's my friend, and I love him! So, fuck you all! When he's on my shoulders I stand tall!"

At five o'clock, I got Jerry from his cage, and put him on my shoulders as I rode my bike over to Olivia's house. Jerry stayed on my shoulders the whole way, and I felt so proud as people turned their heads on the sidewalks, to see a magpie riding with me on my bike!

When I arrived at Olivia's house, Bryce answered the door and said Olivia would be right down. I tucked Jerry inside my jacket and waited.

"I'm glad you haven't brought your wild magpie with you, Kingsley," Olivia's mother said, looking me up and down and then giving me her smile of approval. I didn't tell her he was stuffed inside my jacket, and I was relieved he didn't make any squeaking noises. Bryce, having seen me put Jerry in my jacket, looked at me and laughed.

Olivia finally came down from her room, and she looked lovely this evening, with her tight jeans and fluffy sweater. She had curled her long chestnut hair, 'just for me', her mother said, as Olivia's deep brown eyes sparkled and danced with mine.

"You two behave, and don't have her back late, Kingsley," Mrs. Morris said, as she closed the door behind us.

We walked from Olivia's house on Foxhole Drive to the village in Southgate. From there we walked down Bendrick Drive to the path that led to Pennard golf course. Once we were on the golf course, Olivia reached out and took my hand. I felt like a Prince as I felt her warm hand in mine, and I'm sure I grew a foot taller. Olivia is quiet and gentle spirited like me, and quite shy. We didn't speak much on our way to the castle, but through the holding of hands, we made deep conversation. About halfway to the castle is a meadow of purple heather, and we sat and watched as the late evening sun went down behind Cefn Bryn.

"I have been coming to this meadow of heather ever since I was a little girl," she sighed, and we stopped for a minute to look into each other's eyes. "And do you know, Kingsley, that you can measure the warmth and determine where we are in the Spring season by the depth of the purple flower on the heather?"

"I think so," I replied.

"In the early to mid spring, the flower is at its deepest purple and is most fragrant, and the meadow is full of bees and butterflies.Then in the late spring, when there is less rain and the sun is warmer, the purple flower begins to fade."

"The skylarks also nest in the heather," I said, almost sitting on a nest! "Look, there is a nest with four eggs! I thought as much," I continued to say. "I could see that there was a skylark hovering high above us, and skylark's sing and hover directly above their nests. They will even lure a person away from their nests and babies by flying lower, and then slowly moving across the sky, leading people or animals farther and farther away from their nests."

"That's what I love about you, Kingsley! You are so aware and alive, and you know and feel things that most people don't. And I love your dark curls and green eyes. You are so good looking." At her words my spirit soared as high as the skylarks above us, and my heart sang with them.

"And you are lovely," I smiled. "I have wanted to spend time with you alone, Olivia, and I love holding your hand," I said, as I plucked up the courage to put my arm around her waist. She caressed my arm with her hand which gave me the courage to gently kiss her on the cheek. Wow! I can't believe I did that, I thought, as I looked into her deep brown eyes. And I had the most wonderful feeling, like a feeling of belonging, and I believe that Olivia felt it too.

Pennard Castle is an ancient ruin, built in the late twelfth or early thirteenth century, and was abandoned sometime in the late thirteenth or early fourteenth century we are told. But for Olivia and me, our castle was all we could want it to be, a romantic home for a Prince and Princess. Tonight, as we stood amidst the ruins, my mind became flooded with memories of playing Battling

Knights, and Capture the Princess with my brother Fraser and our boyhood friends.

My mum and our next-door neighbour Mrs. Hall would bring Fraser and me, and Nicolas and Pauline, our neighbour's children here to play. Mum and Aunty Joan, as we called her, sat and read their books, and made a picnic while Fraser, Nicolas and I, pretended to be knights with our wooden swords and shields, while Pauline imagined herself a Princess, and ran and hid in and around the castle walls. Then we boys, I mean 'we knight's' would go and find her and fight each other with our swords to capture her. Pauline was always happy when I won the battle and took her to be my Princess.

"There is one small room still standing in Pennard Castle, and that has always been my special room since I was a little boy. I have always wanted to bring the Princess from the heather meadow here, and make her mine."

"And how are you going to make her yours?" Olivia asked. Her face was blushing.

"By taking her to my room and giving her a kiss," I answered.

Olivia reached out and took my hand, and we walked to the castle room. We sat in the soft sand and gazed upon one another, as the orange glow of the setting sun shone upon our faces and made the castle walls look warm and gold.

As the setting sun bowed his head and tilted his hat to the west, Olivia and I stood in one of the archways that looked out over the Three Cliffs Valley below. The wandering stream looked silver as it winded its way to the sea, which waited robed in yellow and gold for the stream's gentle hand to hold. As Olivia and I listened, the stream began to sing her stories of lovers and friends, who's feet had crossed her sacred waters.

"Will you be my girlfriend, Olivia?" I asked. "You mean so much to me."

"Yes Kingsley, I will," she said shyly as her eyes retreated away from mine.

We stood and watched the silent shouting valley, while Jerry skipped and played in the sand until it was almost too dark to see.

"I can only see his white feathers now," Olivia said. "His dark feathers have vanished into the night."

"Come on Jerry," I called, and he skipped across the sand back into my hands. "Good boy," I said. "It's time to go home." And I tucked him back safe and warm inside my jacket, and Olivia and I held hands all the way back to her home.

"Bye Kingsley, ride safely, and I will talk to you tomorrow at school."

"Bye Olivia, Princess of the Heather, I will see you tomorrow."

There was barely enough light for me to see the road as I rode home through the village. "I'm glad you came with me, Jerry Old Boy," I said, as the dark shadows chased behind us on the bike. "Don't worry Old Boy," I said. "There is nothing here in the dark that isn't here during the day, except for ghosts," I said, as I looked from side to side and peddled as fast as I could go! Thank gosh, there was a streetlight, and the dark shadows began to flee away. "I'm not scared, Jerry, are you?" 'No,' he squeaked, 'but you are.' He was quite right of course. There are lots of ghosts in Pennard. I'd seen quite a few in my time. "What do you think of Olivia, Jerry?", I asked as I raced towards the next streetlight. "She is beautiful isn't she!" Jerry squeaked again from inside my jacket, and said, 'yes, she is.'

Chapter Six

Adams and His Tricks

Tuesday morning seemed to come too early, as all the mornings did when I had to wake up from a sweet dream. In my dream I had gone back to Pennard Castle with Olivia, and yes it was a wonderful dream! I will have to make my dream come true, I thought, as I sat at the breakfast table with my brother and wolfed down my shreddies with hot milk. Today is Tuesday, I mused, and tonight I am going to bring Jerry over to Jeff Adams's house as planned.

As Fraser and I walked to school, Fraser reminded me that Jeff Adams must be scheming some dastardly plan in having invited me over to his place with Jerry.

"You're right, Fraser," I replied. "I may go to Mrs. Morgan's class, but I'm not stupid! I know that Adams is up to something. He has invited Jerry to his house, not me! I will let you know how things go."

It was a typical day at school. George Matthews got beaten up and came into class with a bleeding nose. Our teacher Mr. Davies asked what had happened to his nose.

"I fell, sir," George exclaimed, as he was too afraid of the bullies to tell the truth. Almost everyone in the class broke into laughter as George said he had fallen on his nose. I didn't laugh. I knew how he felt, with the humiliation and fear that went along with the bullying. And as far as

Mr. Davies, and some of the other teachers are concerned, shame on you! You know what's really going on, and you choose to turn a blind eye to it! Shame on you for not doing anything to protect those of us who are vulnerable and abused by these bullies.

At the first break I gave Jeff Adams a football card of Gordon Banks, so that he and his disciples of abuse would leave me alone, although I didn't think he would beat me up today, because I was bringing Jerry over to his house after school. It wasn't just Adams I was afraid of; it was also Andrew Bowen and Mervin Howel, who were part of his gang, and beat me up regularly. But Adams was the leader, and what he said was law.

"Today you can play soccer with your friends, Kingsley," he said, "and no one will lay a finger on you."

"Thanks," I replied, even though it had cost me one of my best football cards.

I played football at lunch break with Fraser, Bryce, and Eli. It was the first time we had seen Eli since our adventures with the toads.

"I'm sorry that I grassed on you," he said. "Die Book and Pencil came to my house, and my Old Man threatened to punch my lights out if I didn't tell him the truth!"

"Don't worry Eli," we all said. "We know what your Old Man is like. And it's all over with now, except for the penance of working in the Staffords garden for the next four Saturday afternoons." At least Fraser and Bryce would have Saturday mornings free. Eli and I would be working on Eli's brother's milk round.

"We will all meet at the Staffords house at 1:00 on Saturday then."

As Fraser and I walked home from school together, he asked me if I was still taking Jerry over to Jeff's house. "He is probably planning to steal your magpie, Kings," he said, "and if I was you, I wouldn't go." For the next few minutes, we walked in silence, as I pondered what Fraser had said. I knew that Adams was up to something, but what? Would he really try to steal Jerry? I wanted to make friends with him, that was the truth of it, or at least not be his enemy. If there was a way I could get him and his fellow bullies to leave me alone, it would be well worth the effort. Playing football with Fraser and my friends today, without having the worry of being beaten up was so nice! I imagined what life would be like if I could have a day like today all the time at school with no bullying. Maybe I would have to give Adams one of my best football cards each week, and then he would leave me alone, maybe even be my friend? But I didn't want to give him my football card collection. I had one of the best collections of anyone in the school!

I finally woke from my daydream and spoke to Fraser. "Thanks for warning me," I said, "but I am still going to take Jerry to his place, I will make sure he doesn't steal him. I just want to try and make friends with him. I'm so tired of him and his gang beating me up."

"Yeah, okay Kings," Fraser replied, "but don't forget, I did warn you."

When Fraser and I arrived home, Mum already had tea ready, and we sat down to eat. "Do you boys have any homework?" Mum asked, as she sat on the other side of the table with her coffee.

"I don't," I replied, lying through my teeth. "I'm going to take Jerry for a ride on my bike after tea." Fraser had homework, and soon disappeared up to his room.

After feeding Jerry some worms and bread and milk, I headed off to the Adams house as planned. I zipped Jerry inside my jacket with his head sticking out in the wind as

I rode my bike through the village. Jerry seemed to enjoy the wind in his face as I sped around the corners and rode fast down the hill past Bromley's Post Office. I was relieved that Eli's brother's dog, Scruffy, wasn't out on the road giving chase. Last time I'd come down the hill on my bike, he almost pulled me off, sinking his teeth into my jeans as I tried to pedal away. Scruffy was a vicious brute of an Alsatian, and should have been put down a long time ago, if you ask me!

Adams lived in a large house on about an acre of fine manicured gardens. His father had been a politician for quite some time, and they even had a butler and cook. No wonder Adams was such a spoiled prick, but I didn't understand what made him such a mean bully. He had this uncanny ability to sense weakness and insecurity in other children at school, and he controlled them through their own insecurities and fears. I was a prime example of this, and so were about ten other boys at the school whom he bullied, but George Matthews and I got it the worst.

I left my bike inside the main gate to Adams's property and walked up the long driveway. I felt nervous now as I saw the house and the front entrance in the distance. What could he really want, I pondered? Only a few of my classmates had ever been to his house. I quickly checked on Jerry who was still sitting comfortably inside my jacket, and then knocked on the heavy door knocker which was a horse's head made of brass.

The heavy door creaked as it opened, and the bald headed butler, whom I'm sure had never cracked a smile, said, "'yes," looking down at me from the end of his nose. "What do you want?"

"I'm here to see Jeff. I am invited," I replied nervously.

"Are you now," he replied in a rather condescending voice. "I will go and see if Master Jeff wants to see you." He closed the door again.

"...want's to see me," I muttered to myself. "You bald headed snob, I'd love to mail you some toads!"

After waiting for what seemed like a long time, the door creaked open again, but this time more quickly. "That was Hobson the butler," Jeff replied, "and don't mind him, if he gets on your nerves just tell him to get a haircut, he doesn't like that, the bald headed coot, and I think he's a bit queer, because he sits down to pee like a woman. Last time I looked he was a man."

I forced a half smile and a chuckle, and then asked, "where is your mother and father?"

"My dad is at a Conservative Party meeting in London, and my Old Girl is upstairs watching Coronation Street. Why do you ask about them anyway?"

"Oh no reason," I replied. "I just wondered," feeling only slightly more secure.

"Anyway Queensley, I mean Kingsley, come on in, let's go up to my room and I'll show you my football cards. And where is your magpie? I hope you brought him."

"Yes, he's inside my jacket," I replied.

"God Strewth! Don't let Hobson know that he's in the house, or that bald headed dick will shit himself. Can I hold your magpie, Kingsley? His name is Jerry isn't it? I hear that he's really cool! Everyone at school is talking about him. Does he really ride on the handlebars of your bike, and sit on your shoulders when you're riding?"

"Yeah he does, he's an amazing bird," I replied. "If you sit down you can hold him." As Adams sat on the floor, I pulled Jerry out of my jacket and put him in his arms.

"Wow! He's so tame. How did you tame a wild bird to sit on someone's lap? He's amazing, Kingsley. Look, he's sitting on my arm now, and he's not scared at all. Oh, here Kingsley, take a look at my football cards while I'm holding Jerry. It's got to be the best collection in the school," he boasted. As I flipped through his cards, keeping a wary eye on him and Jerry, I recognized several cards that I'd given him for my protection at school. There was Roger Hunt, my favourite Liverpool card! And there was Peter Bonneti, Chelsea's goalie, and Johnny Giles and Norman Hunter from Leeds. And there was Gordon Banks's card that I had given him only this morning!

I began to get an ill feeling in my gut. How could this boy who was just fourteen years old, and has so much to be thankful for, use and abuse other people like me? As I looked around his room at his TV and expensive stereo and toys, he had everything a boy could want, yet he was mean and miserable, and delighted in preying on the weak and less fortunate. I kept a close watch on Adams and Jerry now, lifting my head up every few minutes, as I pretended to still be interested in his cards. I could hear Frasers words echoing inside my head, "watch out for Adams, Kings, he's got to be up to something. Make sure he doesn't steal Jerry!"

"So Kingsley," Adams said, with Jerry now sitting on his shoulder. "You are probably wondering why I invited you to my house when we are not usually friends."

"Yeah, I must say I am. I've looked through your cards and you do have a good collection, Jeff.

"I'm glad you think so, my collection is the best." But I knew better. My collection was a mile better than his, I just didn't bring my best ones to school so that he and the other thugs could steal them. Unless I wanted protection that is, and he got the collection he has today by bribing and threatening people, what a loser!

"I want to make you a deal, Kingsley. I will give you my whole football card collection, plus twenty pounds cash, and protection from ever being beaten up again until the day you leave Pennard School. If anyone lays a finger on you or even your friend George Matthews, I will beat the hell out of them!" At Adams's words, my heart sank, for I knew what he was going to ask for in return. Well, I better ask it anyway, I thought, as Adams fixed his cold stare upon me.

"And what is it that you want in return, Jeff?"

Just then there was a knock at the door and it was Hobson the butler. "I just got off the phone with your father, Master Jeff, and he wanted me to inform you that he will have to miss your cricket game. He will be staying in London for longer than expected."

"Damn it Hobson, damn it, this will be the third time in a row that he will miss my cricket game and we are playing for the Cup!" Jeff said, his whole demeanor suddenly changing. "Ok Hobson, what are you waiting around for, Christmas? Shut the door and get the hell out of my room! And what are you looking at Hill, yesterday's flipping news?"

"No," I replied. "I wasn't looking at anything. I am sorry your dad is going to miss your game."

"Yeah, yeah, Queensley, I don't want to talk about it anymore, but you know what I do want?" he replied, with his mean and now cunning smile. "I want your magpie, Kingsley!"

"No, he's not for sale at any cost, Jeff. He's the best pet I've ever had, and I wouldn't trade him for anything."

"Ok Hill, if you don't trade him to me I will beat you up every day at school, and wherever else I see you! I won't accept your football cards or money for protection anymore, and I will also beat up your friends Bryce, Eli, and your brother, and I'll kill George Matthews! It's up to you Hill, you can take all I have offered you for Jerry, and not have to worry about anyone at school. You can be in my gang and be popular for once, instead of a groveler. You can always get another magpie. Come on Kings, what do you say? Come on, let's shake on it."

"No! I'm not trading him, I wouldn't want any other magpie but Jerry! He's mine, and I'm not trading him!"

"Ok Hill, get out of my house!" As Adams raised his voice louder, Jerry jumped off his shoulders to the floor and then skipped across the room to me. I quickly picked him up and zipped him inside my jacket.

"I'm going," I said, "and I never want to see you again, Adams, and I'll see my own way out."

"You will see me again alright, Queensley! I'll be waiting for you at school tomorrow, and when I see you I'm going to beat the hell out of you!"

"Shut up Adams and leave me alone!"

Jeff now stood up enraged, and he shouted, "get the hell out! Get out, or I will stab you with my penknife!" Quickly I pulled open his bedroom door and started running along the landing to the stairs. I kept looking over my shoulders, half expecting Adams to come bolting out of his room. He didn't and I reached the stairs.

"He's not a very nice boy is he," said a voice which made me almost jump out of my skin. I took a deep breath, it was the butler!

"Oh, it's you Sir," I said, with fear in my voice.

"Jeff is a very angry and lonely boy. and if I were you, I would get on your bike and go straight home."

"I will Sir," I replied, already making my way down the stairs, "and thank you Sir."

"Thank me? For what? I'm just the butler, I haven't done anything for you boy."

"I know Sir, I just wanted to say thank you." I reached the bottom of the stairs and pulled open the heavy door.

"Straight home now," I heard him call from the top of the stairs as I closed the heavy door behind me. I took some deep breaths and then ran up the long driveway to the gate. Good, my bike was still there. Glancing back to make sure Adams was not following me up the driveway, I opened the gate and jumped on my bike.

"Come on," I said to Jerry, peeking quickly into my jacket. "Let's get the heck out of here!" I peddled as quickly as I could through the village. Damn it! Old Scruffy was out on the road, and he gave chase! My legs were tired as I'd just peddled up the hill, and I pumped my pedals to get away! Scruffy was gaining on me fast, and I kicked my leg out towards him to scare him away. He sunk his teeth into my jeans again, and it took all my strength to keep my balance on my bike. I kicked my foot out again, and this time caught him on the head. He gave a yelp and backed off. That was close. I thought for sure he was going to pull me off my bike! I coasted now and caught my breath. Jerry was still safe and warm inside my jacket, and I peddled slowly the rest of the way home. I vowed to kill that dog one day, for all the times he's attacked me.

I should never have gone, I thought. Fraser did warn me that Adams was up to no good, but I just wanted to try and change things. Why couldn't Jeff just accept me for who I am? We don't have to be best friends or anything, I just want to be able to go to school or for a walk in the village and not have to worry about being beaten up and bullied all the time. There seemed to be a moment there, just one instant, that I thought I saw a softer side to Jeff. Although I had a bit more insight into his home life now, it didn't change the fact that he was mean and ruthless.

I felt a great sense of sadness as I reached Browns Drive. What was wrong with me? Why can't I ever be accepted by the crowd at school? Why don't I fit in like everyone else? Is it because I am gentle and quiet, and don't fight back when I'm picked on? Is that why I'm bullied, because I don't stand up for myself and punch people in the face and steal their football cards? Maybe I should be mean and spiteful like Adams and his goons. Sorry, Grandma, I know what you taught me, but being kind and gentle doesn't work! Or at least it doesn't work for me. I think I am going to try and become hard and mean and not care about people, at least then I won't be picked on and beaten up at school.

"What do you think, Jerry Old Boy? Do you think I should become hard and mean like Adams and his Gang?" Jerry was silent inside my jacket, as if to say, no, you don't need to change who you are, I like you just the way you are! "Thanks Old Boy," I said aloud. My Grandfather told me that I should never change who I am, or try to fit in to be accepted by people if it changed who God had made me to be. Easier said than done, Grandpa, especially when you are on the receiving end of a fist or a boot. Why don't you preach that in one of your sermons on the fricking mount!

"Sometimes it's really hard to be me, Jerry, but I have you in my life, and that makes me happy, and I want you to know that I wouldn't trade you for all the football cards in the world! Not even for protection from Jeff and the other thugs at school."

"How did it go, Kings?" Fraser asked as I walked through the door.

"Come upstairs to my bedroom and I'll tell you."

Fraser listened intently, and then said, "I'm not surprised, Kings, I knew that bastard was up to something! Look at you, Kings, you're shaking!"

"Adams said he's going to beat me up everyday, Fraser, and he'll be waiting for me at school tomorrow."

"I wish we could kill him for you, Kings! I'd shoot him for you and do us all a favor if I thought I could get away with it. Is Jerry ok?"

"Yes, Jerry's fine, as soon as Adams raised his voice and became angry, Jerry ran across the room into my arms. Even Jerry knew there was something wrong with him. I don't know what I am going to do. He said he was going to kill George Matthews, and even threatened you, Bryce, and Eli."

"If he touches me I'll kill him, Kings!"

"And as if Adams wasn't enough, Scruffy the Alsation tried to attack me on the way home! Sunk his teeth into my jeans and tried to pull me off my bike."

"Yeah, we have got to do something about him. He attacked Bryce and I the other day, and we were just walking by. Maybe we could poison him or something."

"Good idea, Fraser, but in the meantime, I have to deal with Adams. You should have seen the crazy look on his face when I told him that I wouldn't trade him for Jerry. Adams is a mental case, I can tell you that, and he's going to end up killing someone, and it isn't going to be me! I'm not going to school tomorrow, Fraser. I'll pretend I'm having an asthma attack and Mum will keep me home."

"You will probably have an asthma attack anyway after being threatened like that. Remember what Dr.Holmes said. Stress is the worst thing for your asthma."

"You're right Fraser, you know me well my brother."

"I'll tell you what Kings, you stay home from school tomorrow, and I'll ring Bryce and Eli tonight, and let them know what happened, and we will stick together at school tomorrow and see what Adams does."

"Good idea, Fraser, because I'm not going to school. Adams is totally mental. He's bonkers!"

"Oh, by the way, Kings, Olivia called while you were out, and she wants you to call her back."

After talking to Fraser for a few more minutes, I went downstairs and called Olivia. She asked me if I wanted to come with her for a picnic next Saturday evening to Pobbles Beach. Talking to Olivia and knowing that I would be seeing her on Saturday was a good end to a bad day. After feeding Jerry and tucking him into his cage for the night , I asked Mum for one of my asthma pills and my inhaler. I didn't have any signs of an asthma attack coming on, but I needed to fake one if I wanted to stay home from school tomorrow.

Over the years I had become an expert on faking asthma attacks when I was too afraid of the bullies at school. I started getting asthma when I was two years old, and according to the doctors I would grow out of it by the time I was about fifteen. Nervous Asthma they called it, brought on by trauma, although I can't remember any trauma happening to me when I was only two years old. In my childhood, my asthma attacks were devastating and affected every area of my life. Most notably was my lack of confidence and self-esteem, which still has a significant cause and effect today. As time goes by my asthma attacks are becoming fewer and farther between, but their damage to my mental and emotional development has already been done. I look forward to never having another attack again, and overcoming the scars they have left on my soul.

I remember sports day last year. I am without doubt the fastest one hundred and two hundred metre sprinter in the school. I was looking forward to claiming my titles in front of my family and friends, and most of all before the eyes of Lorna Griffiths, the most beautiful girl in the school! I was lengths ahead of my pears in practice and favourite to win both the one and two hundred metre races. Jeff Adams and Andrew Bowen had threatened me to throw both the races so that they could finish first and second in both the sprints, but I refused to give in to their threats. These were going to be my victories, and no one was going to take them away from me! To win the one hundred and two hundred metre races was worth getting beaten up for, but my asthma had other plans, and the night before sports day I had an attack and couldn't compete. Damn you God! If being at the bottom of my class isn't enough, you let me have an asthma attack on the eve of sports day.

I managed to wheeze my way down to the sports field as an observer, and I listened to the other boys and girls saying to each other, "where is he? Why isn't he running? Is he too scared of Adams and Bowen?" And I watched from my hideout in the crowd as Adams and Bowen finished first and second. I don't understand you, God! You must take great pleasure in allowing my heart to get broken. I thought it would be different that year and I could win. One of the hardest things to bear when you are recovering from an asthma attack, is watching other people winning races on sports day that you know darn well, that if you were healthy, you could have won. It hurt real bad.

Well, back to Tuesday night.

"It's time to go to bed," my mother said. "It's a school night, and you need to get your sleep." I had pretended to have a tight chest and to be short of breath, in preparation for putting on the agony tomorrow morning so I could stay home. But my mother always waited until the morning before she made the decision of whether I was sick enough to stay home or not. My real asthma attacks were most often short and mild, now that I was getting older and beginning to grow out of them, just as the doctor said I would. Still a few times however, they started off mild and became more severe within several hours.

"I will see how you are in the morning, Kings. It's important that you go to school if you possibly can. You have missed so much school, and you don't want to be kept behind another year next term do you?"

"Of course not," I retorted angrily. Just the thought of being kept behind again made me feel like such a loser. Lots of people feel sorry for you when you suffer with asthma, but they have no idea how you really feel and what you go through, fricking shitting yourself as you fight for breath and think you're going to die!

Fraser and I still shared a bedroom and we slept in bunk beds, he on the top and me on the bottom. There was a spare bedroom that I could move into, but I liked having company at night as I often had bad dreams. Besides, Fraser and I got on well together, and only fought over food and football cards, and of course girls we fancied.

"Well, goodnight Fraser."

"Yeah goodnight Kings, see you in the morning." And I drifted off into a haunted sleep, thinking about Adams, and getting beat up tomorrow if I did end up going to school.

My dreams of Adams were vivid and frightening, and I got up early and pretended I couldn't breathe to ensure I got the day off. My mother gave me one of my asthma pills, and this time she watched me swallow it. I had managed to flush last night's pill down the toilet. It doesn't do you any harm taking an asthma pill when you're not really having an attack, you just feel a bit light headed. It is a bit different taking a valium, which I stole from my mother from time to time, when I really felt I couldn't cope, only they leave you feeling like a zombie for days!

After breakfast Eli and Bryce met Fraser at our gate as usual so that they could walk to school together. Dad had already left early for work, or maybe he just wanted to get away from my mother, who knows. They had another slinging match last night when they thought Fraser and I were asleep. Mum worked part time now that Fraser and I were getting older, and guess what? She was working today. I had timed it right, and would have the whole house to myself. Not that I intended staying indoors, it was a beautiful day outside and the blue sky and sunshine raised my spirits as I peered out of the kitchen window into the back field. Sensing that my mother was standing behind me, I coughed a few times and held my chest.

"I hope you're not putting on one of your acts, Kingsley," she said. "You know how much that will upset me if you are."

"I'm not Mum," I said, pretending to puff out my words. "I really am sick Mum. I think I am going to lie down."

"You make sure that you do rest," she replied. "If you're home from school then you need to be indoors. There is some lunch in the fridge and I will be home at 5:30."

"Ok Mum, I will see you tonight." I watched from the front window as she closed the gate and made her way to the bus stop. I quickly got dressed, made myself some shreddies with hot milk and wolfed it down. I packed my lunch in my backpack and was off to see the world.

A nice day at Pobbles Beach would be the order of the day, via South Gate Post Office for some refreshers and a dandelion and burdock pop. Oh yes, and a Cornish pasty to add to my egg and tomato sandwich that Mum had made. I opened my savings box with the key which was hidden under my mattress. Being on the lower bunk, one had to climb under my bed to see what was hidden under my mattress, while I could see anything my brother put under his because he was on the top bunk.I took a one pound note from my savings, and tucked the key back under my mattress. A pound would be plenty, and off I went into the aviary to get Jerry. I can't think of a better way to start the day than with a crisp pound note in my pocket, and a magpie on my shoulder! Can you?

Chapter Seven

While the Cats are Away, the Magpie Will Play

It was April the twenty third, almost May, and the song and fragrance of Spring filled the air. The wild primrose and daffodils smiled as I ran across Downes Field, dodging the cow poos, and keeping my eye on the big bull who kept his head down chewing the new grass. Once I reached the safety of the sty at the far end of the field, I taunted the bull, taking off my red Liverpool jacket and waving it in the air. He soon gave chase until he stood in front of the sty before me, digging his hoofs into the ground and thrashing his head back and forth, showing me his big sharp horns. 'One day he will trample you', said my father's words that played like a song in my mind.

Last week he almost got Bryce, while we teased him from the middle of the field and tried to outrun him. We had all walked quietly out to the middle of the field while he had his head down in the grass, just like today and we all shouted together, "Bullshit Bully, come and get us." He was on us like a shot! Eli and I made it to the far side of the field first, jumping over the sty to safety, but Bryce fell right in front of him! Fraser managed to taunt him away from Bryce by waving a stick at him. Bryce and Fraser just made it over the sty in time, as Bullshit Bully thrashed his horns into the wooden sty..

Most people walk around the roadway to get to the village, rather than crossing the bullfield, but this way is about twenty minutes quicker, and that's no bull!

As I continued on towards the village, Jerry sat proudly on my shoulders, jumping from one shoulder to the other and pecking my ears, and getting his beak caught in my long curls that were almost down to my shoulders now. I was going to get a haircut from Eli's sister Debbie last week, but Olivia keeps telling me how much she loves my curls, so I'll keep it long for now. Dad said, 'you know your hair is too long when another boy taps you on the shoulders on the dance floor and asks you to dance'. That hasn't happened yet, so I guess I'm alright.

"Awe! Get out of my ear, Jerry, that hurts! I didn't know you liked ears as well, Old Boy, now stop it!"

We were soon in the village, and I was getting some looks from two old ladies who were walking their dogs.

"Well I never," said one old lady. "A tame magpie, whatever next?"

"Yes I said, my father won't let me have a dog, and my mother is afraid of the frog!"

"Well dear, right you are," the other old lady said. "Have a nice day, you and your magpie too!"

Before going into the Post Office, I lifted Jerry down from my shoulders and stuffed him inside my jacket. "Hello Mrs. Bromley," I said. "I will have 10 refreshers and a Cornish pasty, and a bottle of dandelion and burdock please."

"You're not at school today, Kingsley? Everything alright?"

"Yes Mrs. Bromley, it is now. I had an asthma attack last night and I'm not quite up to going to school."

"Well, it's a beautiful day, Kingsley, and the fresh air will do you good."

"It is already Mrs. Bromley, bye now and have a good day."

Hearing Mrs. Bromley's cheerful words was like having her approval to take the day off. I don't mind if I do, I thought as I crossed the road from the Post Office and walked down Bendrick Drive which ends in the path to Pobbles Beach. I unzipped my jacket and Jerry fluttered up onto my shoulders again. I was always heading for Pobbles Beach it seemed. Rain or shine, if I had the day off then Pobbles was the best place to spend it.

One is never alone at Pobbles Beach, there is always so much to see and do, and during my time off school due to my asthma attacks as a child, the beach became my classroom as I caught fish, climbed rocks, and dreamed in the waves.

"What fun awaits us today?" I said to Jerry, as he jumped excitedly from one shoulder to the other. "Now get out of my hair, Old Boy. Your feet are getting all caught up in it! Only girls pull hair. Now you sit quietly on my shoulder or under my jacket you will go." Jerry seemed to understand the consequences of bugging me on this lovely blue sky day, so he sat content on my shoulder and only occasionally pecked at my ear when he wanted my undivided attention. "What is it Old Boy," I would ask, and he made a little squeaking noise in my ear as if he was telling me how much he was enjoying our day. "I am enjoying it too," I replied. "And if you continue to be a good boy and don't bug me, I might even give you some of my Cornish pasty." He now chirped in approval of our arrangement as we reached the bottom of Bendrick Drive.

At the end of Bendrick Drive is a field which is part of Southgate Farm. And there are several pine trees almost completely engulfed with ivy. There at the top of the pines came the wonderful Spring chorus of the Collar Doves. "Coo - coo - cooh," and their song lifted my spirit higher and higher with their praise of the Spring, and Jerry fluttered and flapped his wings as if he was practicing for the day that he would fly.

Across the field the bluebells were in full bloom, and they swayed in the breeze at us like a sea of waving blue, and here and there were islands of pink and white ones. I would have to pick some of the white ones on the way home and give them to Olivia.

We soon reached the beach path which tumbles along at the side of Pennard Golf Course, a busy course during the Spring and Summer months. As we walked along I told Jerry about my previous job at the golf course. "It was a good supplier of pocket money for us boys who went looking for golf balls, and then sold them at the Pro Shop, 20 pence for a good used one and 50 pence for a new one. Before getting our Saturday jobs on the milkround with Eli's brother Philip, Eli and I made our pocket money almost exclusively by finding golf balls."

Jerry looked at me with his beady black eyes, and I think he knew I hadn't told the absolute truth! "Ok Jerry, I'll tell you the truth," I said. "Stealing golf balls, that's what we did. Now you mustn't tell a soul, Old Boy, not even another bird ok, and I'll tell you how we did it! Come on, stop pulling my hair or I won't tell you!. That's it, you can sit on my other shoulder until we reach the beach. Now listen up. Usually there are groups of two, three, or four people playing together in a round of golf. Sometimes five or six, though not very often as it takes forever for five people to tee off from the tee's and play all eighteen holes. Pennard golf course is quite hilly on most of the fairways, the perfect place for a boy to hide behind one of the hills, and dash out from cover and steal the beautiful shiny golf balls as they come over the hill one by one, and then dash back to cover and wait for the next one. Eli and I took turns stealing the balls, while the other kept a lookout on an adjacent hill and signaled in code. Raising your right hand with a full palm facing out meant the golfers were in position to start driving off the tee. In other words, get ready for action! Raising of the left hand meant that the first golfer had now hit the ball. And how many fingers were held up on your left hand, meant how many golfers there were in that particular group, who would soon be deprived of their brand new Titleist, or Dunlop, or maybe it would be a Galloway today?"

Nervousness and excitement filled my veins as I would wait in anticipation to see the golf balls coming over the hill. Both hands up in the air with palms facing out, meant that there was a stop in the play and to wait for further signals. This was a very nervous time for the 'Golf Ball Thief", for sometimes we were spotted and the golfers gave chase! Then it was everyone for himself! Eli and I would run like the devil to a secret rendezvous place that had been pre-decided before we committed our dastardly deeds. We split the golf balls 50/50, and we usually waited at least a few days before selling them back to the man in the Pro Shop.

We only targeted three sets of golfers per morning or afternoon over the 18 hole course, and we chose our fairways carefully. The 12th, 15th, and 18th fairways had the best hills to hide behind, as the golfers had no angle of view at all as to what was on the other side of the hills. The 17th and 18th holes also had the benefit of most of the golfers being tired by now, and not giving chase if they did happen to see you nick their ball, or put 2 and 2 together, and realize why they had lost so many balls on their round of golf. 2 plus 2 doesn't always make for 4, when you have a thief always wanting more!.

My most memorable experience stealing golf balls was on a Tuesday morning when I was off school with a pretend asthma attack. Eli, along with Bryce and Fraser had gone to school as usual, and I was left with no lookout. It was Ladies Day, and I watched several groups of ladies tee off from the 15th tee before I plucked up the courage to take my place behind 'Slazenger Hill', as Eli and I had named it after stealing 3 Slazenger balls from the same group of golfers. But back to this particular Tuesday.

Over the hill came the golf balls one after the other, and I decided to make a mad dash and try and retrieve all the balls once the last one had been hit. My change of tactics from stealing them one by one was a big mistake. As I was picking up the last ball, I heard a shout from the top of the hill.

"Put down that ball, you thief!"

What could I do? I was busted! I started to run with all 4 balls and tripped and twisted my ankle, as two of the ladies came running after me. I conveniently threw 3 of the balls in a nearby gorse bush, and pretended to have been hit in the head by the 4th.

"What are you doing picking up our golf balls?" one of the ladies protested upon arrival!

"I wasn't picking it up," I said. "It hit me in the head!" And I pretended to cry.

"You poor boy," the other woman said, full of compassion. "Are you alright?"

"Yes I replied, but I will probably have a bump on my head."

"You shouldn't be on the fairway," she said. "Now here's a pound note so you can buy a chocolate bar and a pop if you want, and be more careful next time. You could have been badly hurt! And aren't you supposed to be at school?"

"Yes, thank you," I replied, still holding my head, "I'm sorry for disturbing your game and I will keep off the fairways next time." I got the heck out of there, before the others realized that their balls were missing too! I hid in the ferns at the side of the fairway, until they gave up looking for their balls and moved on out of sight. I then went back to the gorse bushes to retrieve the other golf balls.

"I had 3 brand new balls worth 50 pence each, and a pound note. What do you think of that, Jerry Old Boy? Pretty daring don't you think?" Jerry squeaked in approval. "My pride did take a dent though, pretending to cry in front of a bunch of women."

Jerry and I could hear the sound of the surf now, as we continued along the sandy path to the beach. I always get excited when I hear the roar of the waves. It's like the sea is welcoming you to a new adventure. And it is!

Jerry and I arrived at the beach, and the singing sea was a long way out. Before us was the wide expanse of golden sand, and in the distance the dancing waves sparkled in the sunlight, shouting promises to Jerry and me that this was going to be a special day!

Before you step onto the golden sands of Pobbles Beach, you cross a large mound of wave-worn pebbles that sing a song on the high tides as the surf crashes them about and you can hear them telling their stories as they roll and chatter together in the waves.

When the tide is a long way out, the pebbles song is almost silent as they wait in anticipation for their next adventure in the conquering waves. But if you sit nearby and listen carefully, you can hear them telling stories of their journeys long ago. Sometimes you can find special pieces of driftwood amongst the pebbles, and you can make up your own stories of how and from where they have come.

Today I found a piece in the shape of a snake, and It told me that it had escaped from a zoo in Devonshire, England, and had crossed the sea. The sea was too cold and deep for it to stay a snake and travel across the channel, so it turned itself into a piece of driftwood and traveled far and wide to reach the Gower, where it landed here on Pobbles Beach. "When will you become a real snake again?" I asked. 'When the sun is hot and I'm sitting on a warm rock,' it replied. So I sat it on a rock.

After Jerry and I crossed the pebbles and walked across the sand, I thought I would give him some flying lessons. I pulled him down gently from my shoulders, and held his wings firmly against his body and gently lobbed him into the air. He fluttered like an escaping chicken, but landed softly on the sand. He now skipped in front of me, not wanting me to throw him into the air again. "Come on Jerry," I said. "Just a few more tries," as he took me on a run towards the sea.

He finally stopped running, and then turned and faced me and he pecked me quite hard on the hand as I tried to pick him up. "That hurt Old Boy. I'm only trying to help you learn how to fly! I held him close to my body with one hand, and rubbed his chest with my other, trying to reassure him. This time I threw him a bit higher into the air, and he fluttered for about 20 feet, and then flopped down gently onto the sand. "Well done Jerry," I shouted. "That was better! You flew much further this time. Come on boy, one more time and then you can have some of my Cornish pasty." This time I lifted him as high as I could with my throw, and he fluttered about the same distance. He obviously needed his larger wing and tail feathers to grow a bit more.

We sat down against some rocks and shared my pasty. "I'm a man of my word, Jerry," I said, as he wolfed down the nice flaky pastry. "I can see that it's your favorite too, Old Boy," I said, as he gulped another piece down like there was no tomorrow. "Glad you like it, but that's enough. The rest is mine. Get off," I said laughing, as he jumped onto my lap and tried to steal another piece! I was going to have to find him something else to eat as I hadn't brought any garden worms with me. Just then I saw a sand lice in the sand, and I kicked it towards Jerry. His bright beady eyes saw it immediately, and he wolfed it down. I looked around on the sand for some more, but did not see any. Then I remembered that the sand lice came up out from the sand when the new tide first came in over the sand. That wouldn't help us now, I thought, as the tide was still receding to its low. But how about underneath the pebbles?

I picked him up and headed back up the beach to the mound of pebbles. "Now you sit here Old Boy, and I'm going to lift up some of these pebbles and see if there are any of those juicy sand lice underneath them," and there was! There must have been about ten of them under the first rock. Jerry was on them like Fraser and I are into our shreddies in the mornings, and watching Jerry eat, I think our table manners were about the same. 'A pair of pigs', mother said, but Jerry didn't have a brother to fight over the food, so that made him a bigger pig than I was. "Doesn't it Old Boy!"

"Aren't you glad you don't have a brother to fight with over your food, Jerry?"

"Yes," he replied, wolfing down two juicy lice at a time. "I am!"

"Well, I'm glad you are, my feathered friend, because I'm not fighting over those critters with you."

I had spoken too soon, as I heard a flapping of wings behind us, and another magpie landed on the pebbles about thirty feet away. Jerry seemed quite undaunted by the visit of one of his own kind, and continued to stuff himself with sand lice. "Aren't you going to say hello Old Boy? He looks like a nice fellow, and he's got his long tail feathers too." Maybe it's a male, I thought, and Jerry isn't interested? Who knows? I must learn to speak magpie. Or maybe Jerry was too into his breakfast to notice. As I lifted up the next pebble he was so keen for more juicy lice, that he jumped onto my hand. "Get off Old Boy! I don't want to drop this stone on you, and this one is heavy." The other magpie flew in closer now, and watched with envy as Jerry continued with his breakfast. "Come on," I said to the other magpie. "I'm not going to hurt you, you can have some too." Suddenly he flew up into the air and circled around, scolding me with his cackling call.

"Same to you Old Chap," I called back. Jerry paused his breakfast for a moment and looked up. Our black and white friend started dive bombing us, and then swooped past within a few feet of me, and he continued to scold me with his cackling cry. Just then my soul seemed to understand all the fuss he was making!

"What are you doing so close to my own kind, Mr. Human," he said. "It is not a natural relationship you know! You and a magpie finding breakfast together. We are wild birds you know, not tame."

I sat and pondered for a few moments, just wanting to be accepted by our diving friend. "I will take good care of him," I shouted! "He fell out of his nest, you know," and with my shout he flew away. "Was that your father, Old Boy?" I asked Jerry. "He seemed to recognize you, and even more so, me." Jerry just squeaked quietly and shook his head. Maybe it was a lady magpie.

Discovering Jerry's appetite for sand lice was going to save me a lot of time and effort digging worms in the garden, I thought. What a goldmine of food we have discovered under these pebbles.

Well, it was time to walk on the beach again and discover something else. The tide appeared to have reached its low, not coming in or going any further out. It was just like me, contemplating the day ahead. My grandmother told me that when God had finished creating the sea, he gave it boundaries, telling it, it could only come in so far, and then it had to go out again. And it also could only go out so far too, and then it must sit still for an hour before coming in again. She also said that God had a plan for every person's life, and that plan was made before we were ever born and it was up to us if we followed God's plan for our lives. "The sea doesn't have a choice," she said. "It must come in and it must go out again but you have a choice, Kingsley, because God gave you free will to follow his plan or not." And today, as I looked out across the sands to the distant waves, I wondered if the sea was wondering what it was like to have free will, and decide whether it was going to come in or go out, or maybe sit and do nothing today? In some ways I envied the sea. At least it knew what it was doing! I didn't think that God really had a plan for me. Life seemed to be too hard and its lessons too cruel to believe that he had a good plan for my life. No, if he cared, he wouldn't have allowed me to have asthma, or be beaten up by Adams and his gang! Do you hear that God? If this is your plan, you can stick it where the sun doesn't shine!

Jerry flapped his wings and woke me from my daydream. The sun was rising higher in the sky, and I felt the warmth of its kiss on my shoulders. I decided to take Jerry over to the rockpools that lie to the left of Pobbles Cove. There within the pools was the exciting world of sea creatures for Jerry to discover, and for me to re-discover and befriend again, now that the long grey winter has taken off his hat and coat, and run away over Cefn Bryn.

"Come on Jerry, I want to show you the rockpools and my friends that live in them. Now you mustn't eat all my friends, Old Boy. They are not like the sand hoppers. They have feelings, you know."

First we visited the Dragon Pool. I don't know how the pool got its name, but I often asked my mother as a child. She told me a few good stories, and I believed one or two of them for some time. But as I grew out of my nappies, and pee'd by the rocks like the big boys, I realized that mother's stories were becoming different every time she told them, so I chose to believe none of them. And one day, yes I'll never forget that day, I was fishing for crabs and I saw two little seahorses that looked like little dragons swimming in the pool, and that's how the Dragon Pool told me its name.

There were no dragons in the pool today however, and all was still on its surface as I watched Jerry's and my reflections stare back at us. "Can you see us there, Old Boy? It looks like we are falling into the sky, but don't worry, we're not. That's not really us in the pool. That is a reflection of what we look like. Nature's mirror, I call it. Look, Jerry, do you see what you look like? Now hold on tight to my shoulder otherwise you will fall in!"

Jerry seemed to instinctively know that he didn't want to fall in as I leaned us further over the pool. Suddenly a goby darted across the pool, and a red rock crab moved slowly but deliberately across the sandy bottom, searching for its breakfast, or was it lunch? The crabs and fishes start moving about as soon as the last waves stop crashing into the pool, and all was new and fresh.

"I know what I will show you first, Jerry. I'll show you the Goby Hole, and how to catch gobies." Gobies dear reader are a small fish that for the most part feed on the bottom of the sand and also amongst the seaweed that grows on the sides of the rockpools." As Jerry and I peered into the pool, we could see four or five small gobies feeding on a dead flounder. I once caught a gobie nine inches long which was big for a six year old using a hook and string.

In one of the rock crevices above the tideline, I had hidden some fishing line and some hooks in a waterproof tin last summer, and I climbed the rocks to see if it was still there. It was!

The tin was rusty, and I had to pry the lid open with my penknife, but the hooks and line were still in good condition. "Now look Jerry, this is what we do. First we need to find a rock to smash open some limpets. They are these volcano shaped shells that grow on the sides of the rocks. You can use mussel shells too, but their flesh doesn't stay on the hook as well as the limpets do." As I lifted up a rock ready to bash it against a limpet, Jerry jumped up on my hand again sensing it was food. "Come on Old Boy, this is not for you, this is bait for the gobies."

Lifting Jerry back onto my shoulder, I bashed four limpets of the rocks. I then tied a hook onto the line and climbed back down the rocks to the Dragon Pool. Jerry was quiet as he clung to my shoulder trying to anticipate what I was going to do next. "Well Old Boy, we are almost ready to start fishing. Now you sit quietly on my shoulder and watch."

I pried one of the limpets out of its shell and put some of its flesh onto the hook. The bottom part of the limpet is literally a big sucker which it uses to attach itself to the rocks, and the dark blacky red colour directly under the top of the shell is known as its brain. At Least that is what my friends and I have always called it. The problem with this soft part of the limpet, is it doesn't stay on the shell very well, and the gobies usually take the brain without getting caught on the hook. This is especially true with the small gobies. I tend to put a piece of brain on my hook first, and then add a piece of the limpets sucker to hold it on. That way you have the smell and scrumptious looking brain to attract the fish, and then the harder flesh that stays on the hook when the fish bites.

Jerry watched intently, as I put the bait on the hook and then lowered it about two feet into the pool, right in front of the little open crevice named by my friends and I as the Goby Hole. Instantly there was a bite, and then a strong tug on my line. I caught one, and it was about five inches long. I lifted it out of the pool to show Jerry. He immediately pounced on the goby thinking it was food. He soon realized that it was too big and hard for his beak, but he enjoyed pecking at it and watching it thrash about on the rocks. "Okay, that's enough Old Boy, you are going to get the hook stuck in your beak! And remember, they are our friends, and we don't eat our friends, at least I don't

Old Boy, I don't know about you." I caught eight gobies, and Jerry learned a bit about fish.

It was sure good to enjoy the adventures of spring again, and I looked forward to the summer when I could swim and dive in the sea. After Jerry's fishing lesson, I put a whole limpet on the hook and lowered it to the bottom of the pool where I had seen the red crab. He was still there alright, and he scurried across the bottom of the pool towards the bait. Suddenly he wasn't alone, as a large black fiddler crab stole the limpet and carried it off with his claws. The crab held onto the bait tightly as I gently lifted it to the surface, and then flipped it onto the rocks. Jerry tried to jump onto the crab who pinched him hard on the beak. Jerry squealed loudly and backed off. "You have to be careful with fiddler crabs, Old Boy. They can pinch you very hard!" Jerry hopped up onto the safety of my lap, and tilted his head from side to side watching the aggressive crab move his claws up and down into the air and warning both of us not to come near. Jerry jumped down from my lap a few times to take a closer look at the crab. As soon as Jerry came too near, Mr. Fiddler Crab lifted up his claws in defence and Jerry thought better of it and scampered back onto my lap.

"Wise choice, Old Boy," I said. "He's got big pinchers any way you look at him, and you have only feathers and a small beak. Until you get bigger, I don't fancy your odds," and Jerry had learned an important lesson. You don't screw with a large fiddler crab when you are just a young magpie.

We spent the rest of the afternoon basking in the warm sand dunes, and I fell right off to sleep. I dreamed about Lorna Griffiths in my class, and I imagined her long auburn hair and blue eyes looking into mine, and then I kissed her lovely soft red lips! Then I woke up. "No not now! I don't want to wake up now when I am kissing her on the lips!" Jerry looked at me and seemed to understand as he hopped around in the warm sand. "I wish my dream was real, Jerry," I told him. "I wish that Lorna Griffiths was my girl."

"One day she will be," he squeaked, and I nodded my head in agreement.

Jerry wasn't ready to leave the warmth of the dunes yet, and he climbed onto my chest while I was still lying on the sand, and he folded his wings and went to sleep. Today had been a great bonding time for us both, and I felt happy and secure in our Man and Magpie relationship in spite of what the other magpie had said.

It was getting late in the afternoon now, and the sun was tilting his hat to the western sky. "One more thing I want to show you Jerry," I said, as I stood up and put him back on my shoulder. While we had been sleeping up in the dunes, the contemplating tide had decided to come in and was now dancing with the pebbles in the cove.

"Come on Jerry!" And he jumped from my shoulders and tangled his feet in my hair, as I ran down the dunes as fast as my legs would carry. "I'm flying, Old Boy, look at me, I'm flying!"

"I see. I see," he said, as he flapped his wings for balance and clung onto my hair until we reached the sea.

At first he seemed scared of the tumbling waves, as they rolled over the singing pebbles up the cove. We were just in time to hear the High Tides Chorus as the swells pushed the rollers higher and higher up the cove, the humps of the swells forming far out to sea, and then riding in like wild horses.

Jerry and I were fascinated by the rhythm of the tide, as one roller after the other sang songs with the pebbles, and we both jumped up and danced. The smell of salt and sea rode on the seabreeze, refreshing my face after the dry warm air upon the dunes. A few times I put Jerry down on the pebbles to see what he would do, and each time he fluttered back up into my arms.

"It's a rough sea, isn't it Old Boy, and you're not ready to go surfing yet. Well, it's time we headed home and pretended that we had been home all day. Can you do that Old Boy, and not tell a soul that we have spent the whole day down on the beach?"

"Yes," he squeaked.

"Good, let's go."

A Day in the Life

The way home from Pobbles always seems longer than coming down to the beach. It's not that climbing up the hill and trudging through the deep soft sand takes longer, it's the thought of leaving such a beautiful peaceful place, and returning to the harsh reality of Pennard School and the bullies. I wondered how Fraser, Bryce and Eli had got on at school today, with Jeff Adams having threatened to harm them because of their association with me. I would soon find out.

When we reached the Bluebell Field at the bottom of Bendrick Drive, I climbed the wooden gate into the meadow, and picked some pink and white bluebells for Olivia. Jerry seemed quite amused and looked at me as if to say, "you are a hopeless romantic."

"I am," I replied, "and you will understand one day when you meet a lovely lady magpie." I also picked some small ferns that contrasted nicely with the bluebells. After tea I will ride my bike over to her house and deliver them to her, I thought, and my heart began to beat faster as I thought of Olivia's smiling face and her beautiful deep brown eyes. "You will understand one day" I repeated thoughtfully to Jerry, as he jumped from one shoulder to the other.

I wonder if Mum will let me out this evening, I pondered. She should let me out for some fresh air if she thinks I've been inside all day. Jerry was quiet, and I wondered if he knew something that I didn't? "I hope she lets me out, Old Boy, because I really want to see Olivia."

We managed to walk through the village without drawing attention to ourselves. The old ladies and their dogs must still be on their afternoon naps, or drinking a cuppa tea.

We reached Farmer Downes field and I rested on the sty as my eyes scanned the field for any signs of the bull. There was no sign of him at first, just the usual cow's chewing the cud and shitting up a storm. "Do they do anything else, Old Boy? Other than eating and shitting. Oh yeah, they make milk, cheese, and yoghurt, that's pretty good don't you think! And I like their milk on my shreddies. And what did you say, Jerry? They make steak and sausages too. Yes they do! Gosh I'm hungry, what about you?"

"Now where is Bullshit Bully? I'm not crossing the field until I know where he is. I hope he is a long way away, because I'm too tired to try and outrun him today." My eyes scanned the far end of the field, and there he was, underneath the big old oak swinging his tail.

"Ok Jerry, it's now or never, he's quite a long way off at the top end of the field, and if he does give chase, we should reach the far fence before he does. I'm going to have to zip you inside my jacket, Old Boy, in case we have to make a run for it."

As luck would have it, he didn't even raise his head as I walked briskly across the field, looking over my shoulders every few yards to make sure he wasn't coming. We reached the fence, and then climbed over the hedge into my backyard. "He must be sniffing out some new flavor of cow poo. I would stick to the regular flavor if I were you, Bullshit Bully! It all smells the same to me, like shit!" And I'm sure I heard Jerry squeaking with laughter inside my jacket.

"I hope you're not teasing the bull, Kingsley," said a voice from the other side of the fence. "And why aren't you in school?" Oh great! It was our neighbor and my mother's best friend, Mrs. Hall, bringing in her clothes from the clothesline.

"Hello, Aunty Joan. I just went to the store to buy some refreshers. I had an asthma attack last night, and Mum said I could stay home and rest."

"She did, did she? Well I hope you feel better, but I don't call crossing the bullfield resting. One day he will catch you off guard, and what will you do then?" I wanted to reply, 'run like heck', but I didn't say anything, I just hoped she wouldn't tell my mother that she had seen me in the field.

I climbed the fence, put Jerry back in his cage, and went into the house. I lay on the couch thinking about my day. Mrs. Hall's words seemed to be playing over and over in my mind. "One day he will catch you off guard, and what will you do then?" Suddenly, I had an idea. No, it wasn't just an idea, it was a brilliant idea! What if I was able to lure Jeff Adams into the bullfield, and he was to trip and fall with Bullshit Bully in pursuit? The more I thought about it, the more I liked the idea, and I began to put a plan together.

I will put down some wooden pegs in the field and run a tripwire between the pegs, and camouflage the pegs with grass. Then, I will challenge Adams to a fight in the middle of the field, and get him to chase me. He will think I'm chickening out as I run away in the direction of the tripwire and he will chase after me for sure. I will get

Fraser, Bryce, and Eli to tease Bullshit Bully right at the time Adams and I are walking out into the middle of the field to have our fight. Adams doesn't know anything about Bullshit Bully being in the field, and he will shit himself and run like hell when he sees him coming after us. I will lead Adams right towards the tripwire as he runs after me, and then I will jump over the wire, and Adams will trip and fall in front of Bullshit Bully. What a fantastic idea, and I can only imagine what the bull will do to Adams when he trips and is lying on the ground in front of him! What a great way to teach Jeff a lesson. We can do it on Saturday, I pondered, because Fraser, Bryce, Eli and I, will all be together working in Mr. Staffords garden, serving our punishment for mailing him the toads. We can challenge Adams to meet us at the field when we have finished at the Staffords. I couldn't wait for Fraser to get home from school so I could tell him my plan!!

When Fraser arrived home however, the day had gone a lot worse than expected. Adams had punched Eli in the face at lunch break, and given him a black eye! "Adams is mental, Kings, and he is going to get you tomorrow!"

Fear began to grip me as I listened to Fraser's words. "I will just have to fake another asthma attack," I replied. "I'm not going to school tomorrow if that nutcase is going to be there!"

I told Fraser my plan for Saturday, and he said, "count me in, and I will go over to Eli's house right now and tell him the plan."

"Thanks Fraser, and I will tell Bryce tonight when I go and see Olivia."

"Sounds good Kings, we have got to teach that bastard a lesson for everything he has done to us. I will see you when I get back from Eli's."

"Yeah, okay Fraser, see you in a bit." I lay back on the couch and waited for Mum to get home from work.

"Hi Kings, how are you feeling?" Mum said as she came through the door.

"Oh, quite poorly, Mum. I've been lying down most of the day, and I had to take one of my pills at lunch." I felt bad about lying to Mum, but I had to work on getting another day off from school. If Adams had punched Eli in the eye for being my friend, I can only imagine what he is going to do to me. As Mum looked at me with her concerned and loving face, and believing what I was telling her, I felt even worse. What kind of son am I, lying to my mum, who loves and believes in me so much! I wanted to hurt Adams real bad, for all the pain he has caused in my life. Maybe Bullshit Bully will stab him with his horns or trample him to death. The world would be a better place without that bastard!

I asked Mum if I could go out after supper to get some fresh air, considering I had been inside all day.

"Alright, as long as you don't overdo it," she replied, "because I want you well enough to go to school tomorrow." I hoped she wouldn't be talking to Aunty Joan tonight, at least not until I'd made my escape and was on my way to Olivia's place.

Fraser now arrived back home with news from Eli. "Eli is in Kings. He thinks it's a great idea, and so does Debbie, his sister. She is furious about Eli's black eye. She said to challenge Adams to a fight and the winner of the fight would get 100 football cards from the loser, and then he will show up for sure, although I don't think you will need to give him anything. He hates your guts for not trading him Jerry."

"That may be true, Fraser, but Eli's sister has got a good idea, you guys make him the offer at school tomorrow. Making him the offer might calm him down a bit, and focus his energy on Saturday and the football cards rather than beating us all up."

"I think you're right, Kings, Adams is a greedy selfish twat, and won't be able to resist a 100 football cards. You're not really going to give him a 100 football cards, are you Kings?"

"No, that's a bunch of bull, get it?" Fraser laughed some more.

"What if something goes wrong and Bullshit Bully kills Adams, Kings?"

"Then he will have done us all a favor, won't he! And besides, he's probably only going to get badly bruised, and shit his pants."

"Yeah, you're right, Kings, and that loser deserves what he gets."

Just then the doorbell rang, and it was Debbie James, Eli's sister, wanting to speak to my mother. Whoa, that was too close for comfort. I thought it was Aunty Joan, and then I'd be busted for spending the day at the beach!

"Come in Debbie," my mother said. "I heard what Jeff Adams did to Eli. Some kids were talking about it at the bus stop when I got off the bus. It's just terrible what Jeff Adams is doing terrorizing these boys!"

"Yes it is," Debbie replied, "and the teachers won't do anything about it! A lot of what Jeff Adams gets away with is related to his father being an **MP**."

"I agree with that," my mother replied, "and if that was one of our kids bullying the other kids, we would soon hear about it!"

"Well I'll tell you this, Mrs. Hill, until something is done about Jeff Adams, and I receive an apology from his parents and the school for Eli's black eye, I'm keeping Eli home from school."

As I listened to the conversation, I became more determined to put my plan into action. We were gaining more and more support for something to be done about this out of control bully!

"There is another thing you need to know Mrs. Hill," Debbie continued. "I thought you should know that Jeff Adams is going to beat up Kingsley as soon as he comes back to school."

"Did you hear that Kingsley?" my mother said.

"Yes Mum, I heard, but no one ever does anything about Adams beating us up!"

"Well I'm going to do something! Enough is enough! I'm going to keep you home from school too, until Debbie and I have talked to the teachers and the Headmaster about Jeff Adams."

Well 'happy day', I thought. Now I don't have to fake another asthma attack to stay home from school tomorrow. I now spoke to Mum and Debbie, and said, "It's about time you talked to the teachers, and the Headmaster, and don't forget to tell them about Mervin Howell and Andrew Bowen. They are all part of his gang, and they will be as mad as heck that you talked to the teachers. Last time I told Mr. Richards, our Art teacher that Jeff Adams and his gang beat me up, the following day, they all came looking for me and punched and kicked me in the head, and Adams said that if I ever said anything again, he would cut me to pieces with his knife!" At my words Debbie began to weep, and my mother hugged her in her arms and consoled her.

I felt sorry for Debbie. Eli's mum had died about three years ago, and Debbie had taken on the role as mum as well as being a sister to Eli, and their Father spent most of his time at the pub or gambling their money away on the horse racing, and he was often drunk and abusive to

Debbie and Eli. After receiving the support she needed from my mum, Debbie headed home, and I sat down at the table and had tea with Fraser.

"It sounds like mum has given you the day off school tomorrow, Kings, you lucky beggar."

"Yeah she has. I can only imagine what would happen if I did go to school!"

After supper I got the bluebells I had picked for Olivia, and cycled over to her place. Bryce answered the door and was pleased to see me as always. "Where's Jerry?" he asked.

"Oh, I left him at home tonight because he's tired out. I took him to the beach today and gave him some flying lessons. And you were right about his wing and tail feathers needing to be longer before he can fly. He did try when I threw him into the air, but he could only flutter off the ground for about twenty feet before landing on the sand. I don't think he will be able to fly properly for at least another few weeks." Suddenly I remembered to tell Bryce about the 'so called fight'. I looked around to make sure no one else was listening. "There's something important going down on Saturday Bryce, but I won't be at school tomorrow so Fraser will fill you in," I whispered so no one else would hear.

"Got it," Bruce said before raising his voice again and winking. "Well come in, Kings, and I'll call Olivia. Bluebells hey, it must be love!"

"Yeah, yeah, get out of here man! Where's Olivia?"

"Olivia!" Bryce called from the bottom of the stairs. "Kings is here."

"Ok," she called back. "I will be down in a minute!" Bryce waited with me in the living room for Olivia to come downstairs.

I often wondered what Bryce thought about me dating his sister. He never said a word about it so I figured he was alright about it since Olivia and I were a year older than him.

"So where are you going with Olivia? Bryce asked.

"Yes, where are you taking my daughter, Kingsley?" said Mrs. Morris, coming in from the kitchen.

"Hello Mrs. Morris," I replied, feeling a bit nervous. "How are you?"

"Oh, can't complain, Kingsley, can't complain, and thanks for asking. And who are the bluebells for? Me?"

" No, they are for Olivia," I replied, "but I can pick you some too if you like."

"I'm only teasing you Kings. Don't be shy, and I'm sure Olivia will love the bluebells. I put the bluebells back inside my jacket to surprise Olivia on our walk.

"It's been a lovely Spring hasn't it, Kingsley," Mrs. Morris continued.

"Yes," I replied. "It has been lovely, and I thought I would take Olivia for a walk to the castle this evening."

"That will be a lovely walk! Just make sure you don't have her back late, as it is a school night. And be careful around the horses. The mares are pregnant or have foals already, and the stallions can be quite aggressive."

"Yes, we will be careful, Mrs. Morris."

Olivia came down from her room wearing a lovely burgundy dress and a matching cashmere sweater. Her eyes sparkled as she smiled at me, and I began to feel excited inside.

"You look lovely!" I exclaimed, with an excited tremble in my voice.

"And where do you think you're going, to a dance?" her mother teased.

"No Mum," Olivia protested. "I just want to look nice for Kingsley."

"Well, Kingsley is right, you do look lovely! Now you two have a nice walk, and don't be late." Bryce laughed and went up to his room, while Olivia and I headed out.

"You look lovely," I said again, feeling nervous and trying to fill the silence. I looked into her deep brown eyes and could smell her faint perfume in the air. Olivia seemed shy and didn't answer, but her blush and gentle smile, spoke what words could not. She had even curled her hair for me.

"You look so handsome, Kingsley," she said, and took my hand.

We walked proudly through the village as if announcing our couple status before any passersby, and then we cut across the golf course towards Pennard Castle. Feeling Olivia's hand in mine made me feel like a Prince, and I walked tall and proud.

"I can feel you trembling," she said quietly, almost in a whisper.

"It's because you rock my world," I replied. Instantly her blush grew to a deep pink across her face, as she smiled broadly, and her eyes danced with mine for a few moments and then retreated. I let out a silent breath, as I pondered all that her dancing eyes had said.

We walked over the hills in a knowing silence which spoke so loud. Our souls listened and said things, and I no longer had to wonder how she felt about me. I could feel it in her hand. Her gentle touch and caress of my fingers permeated deep into my soul and said, "I know you, Kingsley." And my heart answered back, and said "I know you too."

We reached the castle grounds and sat on a hill overlooking the valley. We could see a large herd of horses in the valley, with several mares and their foals drinking from the stream. And there on another hill overlooking the herd was a stallion.

"Look!" I said. "He's huge! He must be the dominant stallion."

"Will he attack us?" Olivia asked, as a look of concern grew upon her face. "A friend of mine was charged and attacked by one of the stallions."

"No he won't attack us," I reassured her. "They will only usually charge when people come too close to the pregnant mares or their foals. Stallions are also territorial, and will chase other horses from different herds if they come within their territory. Just like I will charge any other human stallion who comes too close to you!" Olivia laughed and blushed at my words. "Don't worry," I replied. "I may be territorial, but I'm not possessive."

"Oh, but I want you to be a bit possessive, but not jealous," she smiled.

"Alright, I'll charge but not attack! How's that?"

"Perfect," she laughed.

As we continued to watch the stallion, we could see that he was aware of our presence, but he remained where he was, on top of his lookout hill. It was such a beautiful evening, as the westering sun tilted in the sky, and began to light up the hills and valleys with an orange glow. The Three Cliffs Stream winded its way along, shining like polished silver until it shook hands with the purple sea. I pulled out my bluebells from underneath my jacket and gave them to Olivia.

"Oh Kingsley! White and pink bluebells! I love them! You are so romantic with your poetry, green eyes and curls."

I held Olivia's face in my hands and kissed her, as the gentle breeze blew Springs fragrance all around us. Her hair was as soft as her cashmere sweater, and her kiss and the taste of her lip balm excited me.

"Hold me tight, Kings," she whispered upon the jealous wind. "I missed you so much."

Just then we heard the stallion neighing loudly upon his hill. He shook his head and stamped his feet, and then suddenly, he was off, thundering down the hill to the sand dunes, chasing another horse down through the valley and out to the bay. The horse had come up the valley from the beach and crossed into the stallions territory.

"The other horse will have learned its lesson now," I said.

The light was fading fast as the night clouds marched across the sky, and announced that they would be drawing the curtains of the day. It was time that Olivia and I were on our way. As we stood up ready to leave we heard the galloping of hooves.

"Stay still," I said. "We don't want to spook him. Let's wait until he's back on top of his hill." We watched as he galloped through the dunes, zig zagging his way up to the top of his hill, where he resumed his lookout position.

"What if he chases us, now that he has already given chase to the other stallion?" Olivia said, with a concerned expression on her face.

"He won't," I replied. "We are not threatening him and we are a long way from his herd. Come on, walk with me, stand up tall and show that you are not afraid." I reached out and took Olivia's hand. "Let's just keep walking and not stare back at him. Even if he regards this as his territory, it is unlikely that he will chase us because we are already walking away. If you show fear, a stallion can pick up on it, and sense what a person is feeling. I've proved it many times."

Once we were quite a distance away from the stallion, I said to Olivia, "I've also been chased many times too!"

"Now you tell me!" Olivia said, slapping me on the back, and we both laughed.

We walked along the side of the golf course until we reached the bottom of Bendrick Drive. As Olivia waited at the wooden sty, I climbed over into the meadow and picked some bluebells for her mum.

"Oh, that's so nice of you Kings," Olivia said. "Mum will love them. She prefers wild flowers rather than the ones you buy in the stores."

As we entered Olivia's house, I noticed a burning cigarette in the dark room just left of the front door. I stopped to look, knowing that Olivia's mother didn't smoke. Olivia walked back to where I was standing at the entrance of the room and quickly took my hand, she then led me to the living room where Mrs. Morris was busy mending clothes on her sewing machine.

"What's wrong?" I asked, feeling the tightness in Olivia's grip on my hand. She didn't answer.

Finally, after a long pause, she said, "aren't you going to give mum the flowers you picked for her?"

"Yes," I replied, and I walked over to where Mrs. Morris was sitting. "These are for you, Mrs. Morris," I said, handing her the bluebells. "Thank you for allowing me to take Olivia for a walk to the castle," I said.

"Oh, you picked some for me! I love wild bluebells, Kingsley, thank you very much! The white and pink ones are quite rare, you know, and thank you for having Olivia back in good time."

"You're welcome Mrs. Morris, and I'm glad you like the flowers." As I looked closer into Mrs. Morris's face I was instantly troubled, as her eyes told me a sad story. She had been crying, and she had a swollen eye, and the look of sadness and despair on her face, said so much more.

"Thank you again for the flowers, Kingsley, you really are a special young man. I will let Olivia see you out, and I look forward to seeing you again soon."

"Yes, thank you, Mrs. Morris," I said uneasily.

"Bye Kings," Bryce shouted out from his bedroom. "See you soon Kings!"

"Yeah, see you, Bryce. Chicken on a Hedge, mate!" I shouted out, knowing that it was Bryce's favorite saying.

About two weeks ago we went for a bike ride and saw this chicken sitting on the top of a hedge. Bryce had almost fallen off his bike laughing, as we watched an old woman calling and shouting for this chicken to come down from the top of a hedge.

As I hugged and gave Olivia a quick kiss goodnight, she clinged to me not wanting to let me go, only this was not romance, but fear! I could feel her trembling, and the look on her mothers face had said it all.

I reluctantly climbed onto my bike and peddled through the village for home. Olivia's mum was being abused, I was sure of it. What kind of monster would hit a woman? And what about Olivia, was he abusing her too? I then thought of Bryce. He would stand up for himself wouldn't he? Maybe not! His father, who we nicknamed 'Black Morris', was 6'4 inches or bigger, and built like Bullshit Bully!

Bryce had a love and appreciation for the outdoors, more than my best friend Eli did. And when we were all out together, there was this awareness between us, that I had chosen Eli to be my best friend over Bryce, even though in so many ways, Bryce and I were closer and understood each other more than most people ever could. Bryce was always very gracious to me, when the conflict of choosing one of them to do something special with me occurred, like on my birthday, when my Dad told me that I could choose one of my friends to come flying with us up in his glider at the aerodrome. I know Bryce felt hurt when I chose Eli, but he never held it against me, and chose me to do that "special something" with him on his birthday.

Between the four of us, which included my brother Fraser, it seemed to be written in 'Tweenage Law', that one could only have one best friend at a time, and if you threw a girl into the mix, things got even more complicated. Liking Olivia definitely complicated things but I think the main reason that I chose Eli over Bryce, was because we could get into trouble more readily, and get away with it more often. Bryce's father, Black Morris was a force to be reckoned with, and Bryce, and anyone else who went to his house was afraid of him. Seeing Mrs. Morris's face this evening helped me to understand more as to what Bryce and Olivia had to deal with. There would have been no way to get away with stuff with Black Morris around.

After saying goodnight to Fraser, and making sure that my mother had not changed her mind in keeping me home from school tomorrow, I headed up to my room for the night, haunted by what could be happening at the Morris house. It was a fitful sleep at best.

In the morning Fraser and I talked about our plans for Saturday, and how we hoped his day would go at school

"I will make Adams the offer for the football cards to the winner Kings, to persuade him to come and fight you in the bullfield on Saturday. I will tell you what he says when I get home from school."

"Yeah, you be careful Fraser, hopefully he won't try beating you or Bryce up today."

"Not if he gets a chance to fight you for a hundred football cards Kings! He will probably be nice to us until his adventure with the bull on Saturday."

"You're probably right, Fraser, I will see you when you get home from school."

"Yeah, see you tonight Kings, and have a good day with Jerry."

Well, I had another day off school, thanks to Adams giving Eli a black eye and then threatening me. What shall I do with Jerry today, I wondered. Maybe I will take him to Pobbles Beach again, and turn over the pebbles for sand hoppers. That will save me from digging worms in the garden. No, I think I will go trout fishing at Ilston Cwm instead. I'll take Dad's big net too, as well as my fishing rod, and Jerry can play on the riverbank while I fish.

As soon as Mum had left for work, I went into the back yard and started digging worms for bait. What happened to my break from digging worms, I muttered to myself as I thrust the shovel into the soil. Every time I pushed the shovel into the ground, Jerry jumped on top of it, hoping to snatch the worm before I could pick it up and put it in the bait bucket. "Oh do get off the shovel, Old Boy! I'm going to end up slicing your head off, and we're not going to have any worms for fishing at this rate." After Jerry had eaten about ten worms, I put him back in his cage while I just got enough for a morning's fishing. I was tired already with all this digging.

Mom had made me lunch before she left for work, so with Dad's net in one hand and my fishing rod in the other, and with Jerry jumping around on my shoulders, off we went to Park Mill village. Once through the village we reached the entrance of Ilston Cwm's, which is right next to old Park Mill School. Park Mill School was my very first school, and one that I didn't have bad memories of being bullied in, rather there were fun rambles in the woods, and sitting beside the Illston Stream and watching the big trout underneath the old stone bridge. And it was the place where I was first kissed by a girl!

Susan Simmons came up to me on the bridge one day, and pushed her tongue into my mouth before even saying hello. And that was at the tender age of eight. She called it French Kissing. Darn right uncivilized if you ask me, no wonder the British don't like the French very much! I have however learned a bit more about kissing since that forced entry of my first kiss. Three weeks later Susan Simmons' sister Sandra, also kissed me on the old bridge of Park Mill School, but she said hello first! And I even stuck my tongue in her mouth, and our tongues danced together until our teacher Mr. Hollows caught us, and said, 'stop that right now,' and both of you must come and see me after school. I was sure that it wasn't for an encore, and it wasn't! I didn't realize at eight years old that tongue dancing was such a crime! I much prefer kissing Olivia anyway, because it's on my terms, and the tongue dancing is a mutual waltz.

Later on in my life, I found out that Susan Simmons died on the back of a motorcycle when she was only sixteen, and I often wondered how many boys she kissed after me. Lots I hope! Enough to fill a lifetime that she never had.

"Come on Jerry, I'll show you my old school yard. Then we will go up the Cwm and catch some trout."

I REMEMBER THE DAYS OF PARK MILL SCHOOL

I remember the days of the Old School Yard where I dreamed a lot. Where the boys played marbles and conker's under the falling yellow leaves of the sycamore, and in the Spring the pretty girls swirled and danced in their pretty dresses, and made daisy chains on the lawn. They sang and skipped over skipping ropes, singing songs about us boys, and when I heard them singing my name my heart changed its beat and made a noise!

The birds sang so sweetly in the trees, and robins and swallows nested in the ancient storytelling walls above the laughing stream that changed its name on the other side of the bridge where I stood between two worlds.

Ilston Stream was on the right side of the bridge, and the water that ran underneath the bridge to the other side was called Park Mill River. And I stared over the bridge as a six year old and wondered what magic filled the waters. There were black eels and rainbow trout, and dipper birds that seemed to dance on every stone before dipping their heads under the water. On the Ilston side of the bridge was a gate which led to where us children were not allowed to go. It was a world called Ilston Cwm's, where there was a strange Fir Wood, and an even stranger Old Man who had no home and lived somewhere where no one knows. And then there was the Unicorn! The strange horse with the horn on its head, watchout Susan Simmons said, if it catches you you 're dead! But her sister Sandra said, don't listen to her, she is playing with your head. Come here and sit with me, and I'll kiss you instead.

Several of the teachers said they had seen it, a strange horse with a horn on its head, and they had heard the voices of the little people that lived in Fir Wood, so Susan Simmons had said, and I dreamed every night of the unicorn when I went to bed, and mother said, you must not listen to that girl who puts these thoughts inside your head.

The Old School Yard was a place where innocence lived and bred, and good always won the battle over evil even when the morning sky was red. Come over here, Kingsley, I want to kiss you in my bed!

Chapter Nine

Up the Cwm's

"Well Jerry Old Boy, shall we head up the Cwm's? Come on, stop pecking my ear!" For the first ten minutes or so, the path to the Cwm's runs close to the river's edge, and dandelion and cotton seeds race along the bubbling waters like boats in a regatta. The River song grows faint and then silent, as one rambles towards Fir Wood. Soon the path reaches the first of several bridges that stand watch over the beautiful, but now smaller stream.

"Look Jerry!" I said, as I peered over the edge at several trout that were feeding on the surface on a hatch of black flies. Jerry fluttered and jumped impatiently on my shoulders, while my heart began to beat fast at the sight of those lovely trout, jumping after the flies! "Let's set up here, Old Boy, and see if we can catch one of them."

Opening my fishing box I quickly tied a bait hook to my line. "Get out of my fishing box, Jerry, otherwise you are going to get caught on a hook! Here you are, you can eat a few of these worms, but the rest we need for bait." I used a float with a two and a half foot leader, as the river was only about four feet deep.

I made my first cast, or lob to be more precise, as there were two large hawthorn bushes growing on each side of the stream which limited my space to cast from the bridge. I watched in anticipation as my float carried the line right over to where the trout were feeding. One of the trout took my worm and line immediately, and I lifted the top of my rod gently. He was hooked and made a run down stream with the current. Only having a six pound test line, I couldn't pull too hard or he'd snap me off. Holding my rod tip high,I kept the tension on him and allowed him to run. He soon tired and I wound him in slowly and over to the side of the stream. I then carefully lifted him up from the stream and landed him on the bridge, where Jerry pounced on him.

"Steady on Old Boy, you must be as excited as I am! It's not a giant worm, it's a fish." I managed to get the hook out of its mouth while Jerry continued to peck at its flapping body. "You should have been born a bird of prey, Old Boy, like an eagle or a hawk, pouncing on a fish like that." Finally the trout stopped flapping and Jerry left it alone.

Inside my fishing box were some brightly coloured lures and feathers that I hadn't tied hooks on yet, and Jerry amused himself for several minutes, pulling most of my flies out of the box and onto the bridge. Grabbing a plastic bag I wrapped up the fish and then started to put the flies back in the box. As quick as I could put them back, Jerry pulled them out again, and I had to zip him inside my jacket until I had everything organized for my next cast. This time I caught a smaller trout, but it fought like a big one, and I had to play it until it was tired and came up on its side. "This one is a brown trout," I said to Jerry, who was flapping his wings inside my jacket trying to get out. It is a sure fact that magpies are attracted to bright colours and shiny objects. By the time I'd set up for my third cast, Jerry had pulled everything bright out of my fishing box again. "I don't suppose you are going to clean up the mess, are you old boy? No, I thought not!" My next cast was not so successful, as I caught my hook and line on one of the hawthorn bushes, and I lost my worm and hook. I tied another hook on the line and tried again. I could have tried a fly or a feather, but as my Dad often said, 'if it's working don't change it'.

This time my lob was a good one, and the worm landed right in front of some trout. Again a larger trout grabbed the worm and made a run down stream. He seemed to have taken the hook well, so I played him until he was tired and then lifted him out the stream and onto the bridge. He jumped and flapped on the line as I lifted him up, and I was relieved when I finally managed to get him safely onto the bridge! This time Jerry didn't bother much with the flapping fish. He must have discovered that he is not an eagle or a hawk, and that he much prefers worms than the fish they are caught on, so I gave him a few more worms.

Jerry and I spent the whole day at Ilston Cwm's, and I caught four more trout in the deep corner pools where the river turns direction and the current runs slower. We even caught a black eel using my fathers net, and Jerry pecked it and chased it for a good half an hour. It was fascinating to watch him play, as he would allow the eel to almost get back into the water, and then he would drag it back again with his beak and pull it across the stones and onto the grass again. As Jerry played with his wiggling and twisting friend, I took my shoes and socks off and paddled in the river. I have always enjoyed the feeling of the fast water racing between my toes, and the sound of the river singing all around me.

Over the last few days Jerry and I had become great friends, both with our own peculiar ways of looking at life, but we were both learning to appreciate each other's differences. A boy and his magpie; a rather unusual friendship I must say, but one that was becoming wonderfully exciting!

It was time to head home and see how Fraser had got on at school. Had Adams taken the bait of the football cards? And had he tried to harm Fraser or Bryce? Eli had stayed home today and nursed his black eye so he at least was safe. "Come on Jerry, let's gut these fish and head home." As I pulled the guts out of the fish, Jerry wolfed it down like it was caviar. Maybe the fish guts tasted as good as the sandhoppers. Magpies, being members of the crow family, will eat meat and carrion. "I am so glad you are not a vegetarian Old Boy, or a vegan like that skinny family that lives down the road. Dad says the daughter is so skinny that when she turns sideways you can't see her." Jerry squeaked with laughter and we headed home.

Fraser was arriving home from school just as Jerry and I got back. "How did it go, Fraser?"

"Adams took the bait alright, Kings, and he's already boasting around the school how he's going to beat the hell out of you on Saturday. He's a mental case, Kings! And you were right about the football cards, they were a good deterrent in stopping Adams beating me or Bryce up, at least until after the fight that is. Who knows what will happen then. Oh, and Eli's sister Debbie came into the school today to see Mr. Emlyn the headmaster. I bet it was about Adams beating up Eli and giving him a black eye."

"Let's hope the teachers do something about it, Fraser, because so far no one has given a shit about what that nutcase has done to people!"

"I did notice, Kings, that during the last break, the playground prefects were watching Adams pretty closely."

"Prefects, my arse! They are just as scared of Adams as anyone else is. No, Fraser, I think the only weapon we have to fight Adams with, is Bullshit Bully! And hopefully he will trample over Adams on Saturday."

"Yeah, you're right Kings, let's hope he does us all a favour."

The rest of the week went by quickly, and Mum said I could stay home from school until she had heard from Mr. Emlyn, that something was going to be done about Adams. Mr. Emlyn finally phoned my mother on Friday afternoon and said he would expect to see me back at school on Monday.

"He better have done something, Mum," I protested. "Otherwise I'm never going back to that school again!"

"Of course he's done something, Kingsley, now calm down. Mr. Emlyn told me that if Jeff Adams ever threatened anyone again he would be expelled from school."

"I will believe it when I see it, Mum. The teachers just turn a blind eye to it, apart from Mr. Richards. He's the only decent teacher in the whole school! I wish I could go to another school, Mum. Being bullied is half the reason I can't learn at school, and it brings my asthma on too!"

"Let's just see what happens on Monday, Kings. If they don't do anything to change his behaviour, I will keep you home until they do."

"Thanks Mum, I love you."

"I love you too, Kings."

After tea, Fraser and I rode our bikes over Eli's house to see how he was doing. His sister Debbie answered the door and invited us in.

"Come in boys, Eli will be pleased to see you." Apparently Mr. Emlyn had told Debbie the same thing as he had told my Mum, if Adams threatens us again he will be expelled from school.

Eli seemed to be doing better after having had the day off school, and Fraser and I told him how Adams had accepted the challenge of the fight in Downes Field on Saturday.

"We are going to meet him at the field after we have put in our time at the Stafford's garden."

"Sounds like a plan," Eli said smiling. "I hope the bull cuts him up badly with his horns!" After visiting with Eli for a while at his place, Debble said he could come out with Fraser and I for a bike ride, so we all rode over to Bryce's place to firm up our plans for Saturday.

Olivia was out with her mother when we arrived, and Black Morris was still at work. That gave us the house to ourselves. "Come out to the garage," Bryce said. "I have something to show you," and we eagerly followed behind him.

Bryce had got hold of a roll of barbed wire, and had cut a piece off the top of the roll, about 40 feet long to use as the trip wire for Adams. "This will bring that big headed bully down," he grinned. "The barbs will catch hold of his trousers and keep him on the ground while Bullshit Bully tramples on him and thrusts him about with his horns!. Trust me it works, I tried it out in the back garden today while my folks were out."

"Well done Bryce," we all said, imagining Adams lying face down in the field with Bullshit Bully standing over him.

"And I also got these," Bryce continued. "I stole them from the building site last night," and he opened a cloth bag and pulled out twelve nine inch nails. "These will work much better than tent pegs. They are strong and will go deeper into the ground, and will hold the wire a few more inches higher, so that Adams will trip for sure."

"You just better time it right, Kings, and jump over the wire, because once a person gets caught on these barbs they are down for the count, and at the mercy of Bullshit Bully, and somehow I don't think he's going to show much mercy!" We all looked at each other and laughed, and patted Bryce on the back. "I will get punished badly if my Old Man finds out that I was involved in this," he said, "but it will be worth it to see Adams' beat up face."

"Yeah," we all echoed. "We can't wait to see that bully's face all bruised up after Bullshit Bully has finished with him!"

"And don't worry about your father, Bryce", Fraser said. "We are all in this together, and if we get caught we will all take the blame." We all nodded our heads in agreement with Fraser's words, but I was beginning to see what a monster Bryce's father really was, and I imagined Black Morris hurting Bryce badly if he found out.

"Ok," Bryce said. "Let's go through the plan so that everyone knows their job. Fraser and I will set up the tripwire in the field before anyone else arrives, and then hold onto the football cards so none of Adams' gang can steal them. Kings and Adams will walk out into the middle of the field towards the tripwire. And don't forget to look for the three pieces of bright red wool, Kings! They will be at each end of the tripwire and one in the middle so that you will know exactly when to jump over the wire. And Eli's job is to agitate the bull and make sure he sees Kings and Adams crossing the field. Wave your arms and make sure he gives chase before running back to Fraser and I at the sty, Eli, and we will make sure that none of Adams' gang goes onto the field, otherwise the bull might chase them instead of going after Adams and Kings."

"How are we going to stop Adams' gang going onto the field?" Fraser asked. "They would want to watch the fight."

"The deal will be no one on the field except Kings and Adams, or the fight will be called off and no one will get the football cards. Eli will be hiding in the hedge until Kings and Adams are a good way across the field, and then he will wave his arms and provoke Bullshit Bully to chase."

"A great plan," we all said to Bryce, and it was time to head home.

Eli, Fraser and I got onto our bikes and peddled through the village. What a great plan, I pondered, as we rode up the post office hill and I felt more excited than nervous, as I looked forward to seeing Adams at the mercy of the Bullshit Bully.

Chapter Ten

Bullshit Bully

Fraser and I woke up early Saturday morning, but I felt more nervous than excited, other than more excited than nervous as I had felt last night, but there was no backing out now! This was our chance to get back at Adams's for everything he had done to us! That bully needed to be taught a lesson, and today was the day he was going to learn it!

After breakfast Fraser cycled over to Bryce's to help him set up the trip wire as planned, and I went over to Eli's and we did our milkround as usual. When we met up with Bryce and Fraser at the Stafford's garden, they brought back a good report from Downes Field. There were no cows in the field to foul up the trip wire, and Bullshit Bully had remained at the far end of the field, and seemed content grazing near the big oak tree. This was good news because if the cows were in the field they could easily trip on the wire and pull it up, and we would not have time to set it up again before Adams and his goons arrived at the field. Fraser also said that he had seen the cows in one of the far fields, which usually meant they would not be coming down to Downes Field anytime soon, at least not today anyway.

We rang Mr Stafford's doorbell and waited for the strict man to answer. "I'm glad he's not my Dad," Fraser said, just before Mr. Stafford opened the door. "He's got the personality of a stop sign." Eli and I pinched ourselves to stop laughing, as old man Stafford looked us up and down.

"Well, you lot," he said, "have you learned your lesson not to put toads in people's letter boxes yet?" I was tempted to say, 'no we haven't you miserable old cus', but I held my tongue, and none of us said anything. "What's the matter boys?" he taunted. "You're lost for words now aren't you!"

"No, we are not lost for words," Eli answered, speaking for us all. "What do you want us to do today?"

"I want one of you to mow the lawn," he said, "and the other three of you can turn the soil in the vegetable patch, and also do some weeding around the flower beds. I don't care who does what, as long as you boys do a good job. The tools are in the shed like last week. I will be out to check on your work in an hour." We threw coins to see who got to mow the lawn, and then again for who would do the weeding. I won the toss and chose to use the lawnmower, while Bryce got to turn the soil. Fraser and Eli came in third and forth and were relegated to doing the weeding.

Mowing the lawn was the easiest of the garden chores, at least I thought so, and the time went by quite quickly as I tried to keep tight straight lines across the lawn, and I teased the others each time I made a turn. "Put your back into it boys! What do you think this is, a freaking holiday?" Eli laughed and threw his water bottle at me.

"Look out boys, Old Staffordy is coming," Fraser said, as we all tried to look busy again. Staffordy checked on our work with no complaints and headed off to his garage.

"Don't forget to put the tools back before you leave," he said, "and I will see you all back here at the same time next week."

Just as we were putting the tools back in the shed, the local policeman 'Die Book and Pencil' came around to make sure we had shown up for work and were doing a good job. "I wondered when Carrot Top was going to show up," Fraser said. "I bet he's happy we are here every Saturday afternoon rather than stealing apples in the orchard."

"You have got that right," Bryce said. "Now let's get back to Downes field before Adams and his gang show up."

As we left Mr. and Mrs. Stafford's garden, they sneered at us from their living room window. Fraser sneered back at them and said, "they are both looking more like toads every time we see them." I nearly fell over laughing as Eli and Bryce began to make croaking noises, as Old Staffordy continued to stare out of the window to make sure we closed the gate behind us. "Good riddance you old fart," Fraser said, and we were on our way to Downes field. As we cycled along the road we fine tuned our plans for Adams, and I couldn't wait for him to meet Bullshit Bully, face to horns so to speak. We were soon at the field.

When we arrived, Adams was already there with two of his goons, Bowen and Howell. "That's no surprise that they showed with him," Bryce said, and I began to feel nervous again. We all met at the wooden sty at the bottom of the field, and Adams immediately asked to see the football cards.

"There better be a hundred of them," he demanded, "and you give them to me now so I can count them."

"You're not having them now," Fraser replied. "You are going to fight my brother for them first, and only if you win can you have them."

Bowen and Howell looked at one another and laughed. Then they said to Adams, "did you hear that Jeff? If you win!"

"Yeah, I heard, and I'm going to kick Hill's teeth down the back of his throat and get all the cards!" I felt a tightness in my stomach, and a lump in my throat as I heard Adams' words. What if things went wrong? But it was too late to back out now, and I lifted my head up to see Bullshit Bully at the top of the field. '

"I can surely do with your help, Bully," I whispered under my breath.

"What are you doing, Queensly," Adams said, "saying your prayers? You're going to need them because I'm going to beat the shit out of you!"

"So where are you guys going to fight?" Howell asked.

"In the middle of the field," Bryce answered, "so you guys can't break up the fight!"

"It won't need breaking up." Bowen replied. "Jeff will knock Queensley's block off with one punch!"

"The middle of the field? I thought you would want to be at the edge of the field so you could run away you big baby," Adams taunted, looking right at me. "I'm going to kill you Queensley!" My heart began to race and I felt like running already! 'Come on Kings, you can do this', I whispered to myself, trying to regain my composure. I glanced up to the top of the field to where Bullshit Bully was still feeding near the big oak.

"What are you looking for," Howell taunted, "the second coming? Or your guardian Angel? You're going to need one of them, once Jeff has finished with you, Queensly!"

"No, he's going to need a priest for his last rights," Bowen puffed out. Eli now winked and nodded his head at me, seeing that I had seen where the bull was at the top of the field.

"Are we all ready?" Fraser said.

"Yeah, I'm ready," Adams replied. "I'm looking forward to punching your brother in the face and having another hundred football cards for my collection."

"Are you ready Kings? You got this," Bryce replied calmly.

"Yeah, I'm ready," I gulped.

"Ok listen up," Fraser said. "Kings and Adams are going to walk out into the middle of the field. Eli will accompany Kings, and Howell will accompany Adams." Wait a minute I thought. This isn't in the script! Howell accompanying Adams, and Eli accompanying me. I thought that Eli was going to be hiding in the hedge and was going to jump out and taunt Bullshit Bully to give chase! I was just about to speak up and say something to Eli, until he looked across at me with a look that said, 'trust me'!

We were almost in the middle of the field now, and Eli began to drop back. "Come with me," he said to Howell, who now dropped back too.

"What is it," Howell protested. "What do you want?"

"Watch this," Eli said, and he began to wave his arms in the air and shouted, "come on Bullshit Bully, come on!"

"What is he saying," Adams said, looking across at me, "and who the hell is Bullshit Bully?"

"Oh, he's just a friend of mine who wants to meet you," I replied. "I think you will like him." I glanced up to the top of the field again and noticed Bully had his head up and was beginning to run in our direction.

Eli continued to wave his hands in the air and shouted, "come on Bullshit Bully, come on!" The bull was thundering towards us now, and Eli began to run to the side of the field, leaving Adams and I, and Howell just standing there! "Come on Howell," Eli called out. "Follow me or the bull will plough you down."

"I'm not arguing with that," Howell shouted, and started to follow Eli to the side of the field.

"What the hell is going on, Queensly?" Adams said nervously. "Shit it's a bull! To hell with this," and he started running after Howell and Eli who had now reached the side of the field.

"Wait Adams," I said. "Come on you coward, let's race to the end of the field and whoever gets there first wins the cards." Adams looked at me and then the bull, and then started to run towards me. It's working I thought, as I scanned in front of me for the tripwire, Adams is following me! I quickly looked behind me, and the bull was right on us, Adams was catching me up too! Just then I noticed the red wool on the trip wire and leaped right over it. Adams ran right into the wire, and tripped. He was stuck fast on the ground and he tried to get up.

"I'm stuck!" he shouted. "It's barbed wire, and I can't get up! Kingsley, help me please!"

It was too late for help as Bullshit Bully was right on Adams, thrashing his horns into his sides and stamping him with his hooves. Adams began to scream and I stopped running. I tried waving my arms at the bull now, trying to distract him away from Adams, but Bullshit Bully continued to thrust his horns back and forth across Adams' body, and stamped his hooves on top of him. Adams was still ,and I thought he must be dead!

"Help!" I shouted. "Adams is hurt real bad!" Eli and Howell reappeared now from the side of the field, and started waving their arms for the bull to chase after them. The bull wasn't moving, he just stood there standing over Adams' motionless body. Finally, he backed off and began to slowly walk away towards the other side of the field. Fraser, Bryce and Bowen, having seen what had happened now, ran down the field towards us.

"Is he alright? Is he alright?" Bowen shouted, and now arrived on the scene. "What have you done?" Bowen shouted. "He's dead, you've killed him!"

"He's not dead," Bryce said, kneeling down and listening for his breathing. "He's unconscious but he's still breathing."

"Get an ambulance," Eli said, and Howell and Fraser ran to the nearest house to get help.

Adams began to regain consciousness now, and began to scream and cry. "Aww my side! My side! Help me, I have such a pain in my side and I can't move!" Shit, I thought, maybe Adams is paralyzed. Suddenly he began to move his arms and legs. I felt some relief knowing he wasn't, but he was obviously badly hurt.

"We went to the nearest house and they called an ambulance," Fraser said, arriving back with Howell, and we all stood around and waited until we heard the sirens.

"Over here!" I shouted, as we saw the ambulance on the road on the other side of the field. "Yes, over here," we all shouted! Finally they saw us waving and stopped. Two men and a woman arrived with a stretcher.

"What happened?" the woman asked.

"He got mauled by a bull," Fraser said, and we all looked back and forth at each other in silence.

"He's caught in barbed wire," the ambulance woman said. "Who the hell would put down barbed wire in the middle of a field with animals in it?"

"I don't know," I replied, pretending we knew nothing about it. One of the men cut Adams' jeans away from the wire, and asked him if he could move.

"I don't know," Adams replied, "my side is killing me, can you give me something for the pain, I'm going to pass out."

"Try to stay awake," the man said, "and we will give you something for pain in a minute." Slowly they aligned Adams' body until he was lying straight ,then they put a brace around his neck, and gently lifted him onto the stretcher. As the men carried him across the field to the ambulance, the woman asked us questions as to his identity and where he lived. Howell and Bowen were allowed to ride with Adams in the ambulance, while the rest of us stood around feeling quite shocked.

"Well that worked out a lot better than we anticipated," Eli said, trying to break the awkward silence.

"I don't feel sorry for him," Fraser said. "He needed something like this to happen to teach him a lesson for all the people he's beaten up at school."

"Fraser is right," I echoed. "A broken arm wouldn't have taught him much of a lesson. Hopefully he's got some broken ribs and will be away from school for a long time." Bryce was quiet, almost in tears.

"When my Old Man finds out about this, I'm dead!" he replied.

"No you're not," we all answered, although I was not so sure. "He better not lay a finger on you or he will have all of us to contend with," I replied forcefully. Bryce forced a smile and we walked back across the field to our bikes and then cycled quietly to the village.

"I'm going to buy us all a can of coke," I said. "We need to celebrate."

"Yeah," Eli said, "and the refreshers are on me." So we went into the Post Office and then drank our pop and ate our refreshers sitting on the village wall.

"Cheers," Fraser said. "To Bullshit Bully!"

"Yeah cheers everyone, to Bullshit Bully, may he always be in Adams' dreams!"

"You mean nightmares," Bryce said, and we all laughed.

It was my turn to toast now. "Lift a can everyone, to Bullshit Bully! May your reign be a long one, and your penis not a short one. I give you Bullshit Bully, the best bull on the Gower Peninsula! Cheers everyone, cheers!"

After we had finished our celebrations, Bryce suggested that we go back to the field and get the barbed wire and the nails, otherwise we could be in more trouble if one of the cows or someone else got caught in it.

"A good idea," Eli said, and we all went back to the field to retrieve the wire. Once we had pulled up the nails, and rolled up the wire, we all headed home for the evening.

"Shit, that was close," Fraser said, as we arrived at our home. "I thought Bullshit Bully had killed him! Didn't you?"

"Yes," I replied. "I thought he was dead for sure, until I saw him move." I didn't let Fraser know, but I was both happy and tormented at the same time as I pondered the gravity of what we had done.

Adams had sustained a serious concussion and three broken ribs, along with alot of other cuts and bruises, and the tripwire was never mentioned to Die Book and Pencil. I think Adams' pride was just too hurt to admit that he had been outwitted by those he had so often bullied.

Over the next few months, Adams came to school bandaged from his shoulders to his waist, and even wore a neck support and head brace. Bryce thought he looked like Big

Bird on Sesame Street, but Fraser argued he looked more like Frankenstein. Eli said that tossers come in many shapes and sizes, and that wanker was the biggest one of all!

Even now, Lazzarus, which is Adams's new nickname around the school, tried to spread a rumour that he was winning the fight against me before the bull came and attacked him. Fight! What fight? We didn't even have a fight, it was a race to the far side of the field with Bullshit Bully in pursuit! Anyway, it didn't seem to matter what Adams said anymore. The kids aren't stupid, and even Adams' goons knew that he had been truly outwitted by the boys from Browns Drive. Adams' father, being a local politician, made sure that Bullshit Bully was put down, never again to harm any of us precious children, so the papers read. But I know the press got it wrong. Bullshit Bully was the only innocent one amongst us and our hero! And if Adams' father ever becomes leader of the Labour Party, he won't get my vote, putting down an innocent animal like that! He wasn't teaching his son any lessons about 'Pride' was he. My Grandmother says that pride comes before a fall! It sure did in Adams' case, and with a little persuasion from a barbed tripwire and a charging bull!

They called Bullshit Bully a dangerous animal in the newspapers. Bollocks! What a load of bullshit they write in the press these days. He wasn't the dangerous animal, Adams was! The truth of the matter is, Bullshit Bully is my hero, who helped us boys teach a wanker of a bully a lesson that he will never forget. I hereby dedicate this chapter of my book to Bullshit Bully! My friend, and who's name I hope will live on in every BBQ Steak, here in South Wales. I give you Ladies and Gentlemen, Boys and Girls, " Bullshit Bully", cheers now, and pass the steak sauce if you please, this steak is fan-freaking-tastic!

Chapter Eleven

Long John Jerry

Thanks to Bullshit Bully, the playground at Pennard School became a place of peace and enjoyment, the way it should have been, with the absence of tyrants like Adams and his gang. Adams remained subdued and withdrawn for the rest of the term. Traumatized, the counselor called it. And Howell and Bowen, seemed to soften into almost likeable individuals without the sadistic and tyrannical influence of Adams.

Even though Fraser, Eli and I, hadn't got into any serious trouble over our antics with Bullshit Bully and the injuries that Adams sustained, everyone in the village knew about what had happened. Die Book and Pencil did a full investigation, which took into account that Adams' bullying was the main reason why we did what we did, and Adams' father chose not to press any charges on us boys for his son's injuries.

My Dad told us boys that he believes that the reason Adams' father didn't throw the book at us, was because he thought that any further exposure of his son being involved in bullying in the school and community, would affect his chances of retaining his parliamentary seat in the next election! I tend to agree, what else can one expect from a British Labour Party MP, other than another cover up! However in our case Adams' fathers political tactics worked for our benefit and we were not penalized for what we did.

As expected, Bryce's dad, Black Morris, punished Bryce severely! Fraser, Eli and I , were banned from coming over to Bryce's house. This created a challenge for Olivia and I to maintain seeing each other during the weekdays when she had homework. Olivia's mum however, remained supportive of our relationship, and allowed Olivia to come out on walks after she had finished her homework, and of course we were able to see each other on weekends when we could spend full days together.

Black Morris gave Bryce the strap for his part in our Downes Field adventure, and he also found out that Bryce had used his roll of barbed wire. Olivia told me that one day Bryce had stood in front of his mother to protect her, and Black Morris punched him in the face. I had been a witness to that monster's actions, having seen Bryce's black eye the following day. All us boys hated Black Morris with a passion and swore that we would one day take vengeance on that black hearted devil!

Spring slowly grew into summer, and Jerry accompanied me almost everywhere I went. We were always together, like best friends were.

On July the 16th, Jerry learned to fly! For me this would be the ultimate test of our friendship. Now that he could fly and travel anywhere he wanted to go, would he stay with me and continue to be my friend? My heart told me he would, but I reasoned in my mind how this new found freedom of flying might affect us. Maybe he will want to fly away and explore other parts of the Gower? Certainly now that he is growing up, he will want to find a mate one day and have a family of his own. Would he still want to be my friend, when his feathered friends all around him are wild. Oh, I could go on pondering what might happen forever, I thought, and I decided to just listen to my heart. And my heart said, we would be friends forever and would adjust to all the changes in our lives as they came along. There was only one question that I really needed to have answered, and that was, 'did he feel the same way about me as I did about him? He is my best friend! I had also told Olivia the same thing, so I'm glad they don't talk to each other much.

One Monday afternoon, I was sitting in Mr. Richards Art Class, dreaming of the summer holidays, when there came a tap tap tap on the classroom window. One of my classmates, no she was more than a classmate, she was the most beautiful girl in our class, Lorna Griffiths, shouted out excitedly, "Kingsley, your magpie is at the window!" The whole class got up from their seats and raced to the window.

"Back to your seats boys and girls," Mr. Richards said in a loud voice. Once we were all sitting down again, Mr. Richards opened the window and let Jerry into the classroom. "Is this your magpie, Kingsley Hill?" he asked.

"Yes sir, he is," I replied, thinking I might be in trouble. "He must have flown all the way from my house on Browns Drive, Sir!"

"Will he come to you if you call him, Kingsley?"

"Yes Sir he will. Come on Jerry," I called, and he flew from the windowsill to my desk and started playing with my pencils. The whole class roared with laughter and clapped their hands, except for Adams and Howell. They didn't get excited about much at all these days, especially about my magpie.

"Now don't crowd around him," Mr. Richards said. "I will tell you what we are going to do for this lesson. We are all going to draw a picture of Kingsley's Magpie. And everyone gets to ask Kingsley one question about Jerry throughout the lesson today. And for your homework, I want everyone to write a short essay about Jerry." My gosh! Was I hearing this right? I hadn't liked Mr. Richards much up until now, but he just asked the whole class to draw a picture of my magpie and write an essay about him! My self esteem had just risen 100 degrees!

Several of my classmates came up and asked me questions about Jerry, and I answered them all. I had sure learned alot about magpies, I thought, and I could feel my confidence rising some more.

Next thing I knew, Lorna Griffiths was standing at my desk, and she said, "could I come and see you and Jerry after school?"

"Yes," I choked. "Why don't you come and watch him fly! He has only just learned to fly." She smiled and then went back to her desk.

The end of school bell rang, and I walked out into the school yard as proud as a peacock, with Jerry riding on my shoulder. All the other children shouted out to Jerry and I, and said, 'you're so cool Jerry Magpie! Hope you come again! And thank you Kingsley for bringing your magpie to school'.

That was the most fun art class ever! I kept walking until I reached the far end of the school field, where I basked in the warmth of my new found popularity. As I looked back across the school field to the classrooms, I could see Mr. Richards in the playground. That was unusual, as all the teachers usually went to the staffroom after the school bell. Mr Richards now started to walk towards me, having spotted me at the far end of the field. "He's coming towards us, Jerry Old Boy, I wonder what he wants?"

Mr. Richards arrived at where we were sitting, and said, "Kingsley, I have been meaning to talk to you. I want you to know that I have noticed how hard you have been trying with your school work, and your marks have been going up each week. Mr. Davies has also noticed how well you are doing, and we have decided that you don't need to go to Mrs. Morgan's class anymore, so just stay in regular classes starting tomorrow. Well done Kingsley, I'm really proud of you."

"Thank you Sir," I replied, hardly believing what I'd just heard, and as Mr. Richards walked away, I began to weep. All this time I thought I was so stupid, and not able to learn. And look at me now! I don't need to go to Mrs. Morgan's class any more! All I had needed was not to be bullied and threatened by Adams and his gang, and now I can learn as well as anybody else. I had noticed that my asthma was a lot better too. I had had only one bout of asthma since Bullshit Bully had put Adams in his place. "I hope you know that you are a big part of me being able to learn, Jerry," I said, as he played and skipped around on the grass in front of me. "Thank you my great friend. You are the best friend I could ever have," and I knew he understood what I was saying, because Immediately after I had finished speaking, he flew up into my arms and started pecking my ear. "You know that though, don't you Old Boy," I said laughing. "Now stop pecking my ear, it tickles. I know, it's your magpie kiss, isn't it, when you peck my ears." And just when I thought my day couldn't get any better, I could see Lorna Griffiths walking towards us in the distance. "I can tell it's Lorna Griffiths, Jerry, because she and her sister are the only two girls in the school with blonde hair, and it comes down to her waist when she lets her hair down, Old Boy, you should see it! Ok, here she comes, we have to be really cool ok, and not be nervous." Jerry looked at me kinda strange, and said, 'speak for yourself, I'm not nervous', and he flew out of my arms and onto Lorna's shoulder. She screamed at first, and then laughed.

"Kingsley, will he bite me?" she asked.

"No," I assured her. "He won't bite you, he might peck your ear gently, but that just means he likes you."

"Ok Jerry, I like you too," she squirmed as he pecked at her bright earrings.

"Magpies like bright things," I said, "so make sure he doesn't steal your earrings," and I lifted Jerry back onto my shoulders.

"Wow, he's wonderful Kingsley! I would love to have a pet like Jerry." Lorna and I sat and talked in the field while Jerry hopped and played on the grass looking for insects to eat. "Why doesn't he fly off to be with the wild magpies?" Lorna asked.

"One day he might," I replied. "He fell out of his nest when he was a baby, and I have looked after him ever since. But one day I think he will want to find a mate and build a nest, and raise a family of his own." Lorna listened and pondered my words.

Then she said, "I know that you would want him to be happy, Kingsley. You are very kind, and would want him to be able to have a family of his own, even if it meant giving him up."

"Yes," I replied, feeling surprised that she could read my heart as she did. Lorna and I sat and talked for almost an hour, until her sister found us and said that she had to go.

"Gosh look at the time," Lorna replied. "Bye Kingsley, I better go, and thank you for introducing me to Jerry and spending time with me."

"Bye," I said. "I enjoyed spending time with you too."

It had been so nice to get to know Lorna a bit, she really was as lovely on the inside as the bombshell she was on the outside. Some of us boys, no, probably most of us boys had been too shy to even talk to her. As I walked home from school with a spring in my step and a confidence I had never known before, I thought about my life and how good it was. Today had been like a dream and I never wanted it to end! I could go to school now and not have to be afraid of being beaten up, and people wanted to be my friend and get to know me, even Lorna Griffiths! And I had a wild magpie as a pet, who was the envy of all the other kids. "And you flew all the way to school today to see me, didn't you Old Boy! You are so cool, that Mr. Richards whole class had to draw you today, as well as write an essay. So how does it feel to be a celebrity, Old Boy? Hey, stop pecking my ear, I know you're happy. Me too boy! I have two girlfriends now, Olivia and Lorna. What did you say Jerry? I can only have one! Yeah, I know, but can I have two just for a few weeks? Tell you what, when you meet a girl magpie, I won't tell anyone if you meet another one too! Ok? Deal!"

When I arrived home, Fraser, Bryce and Eli were waiting for me, and had already arranged a bike ride to Pennard Cliffs, and of course I was expected to go with them. I think that this was one of the first times in my life that I would have been just as happy to be on my own. I was changing inside and now felt I had other options in my life as to what I wanted to do. I wanted to go and pick two bunches of bluebells and drop one off for Olivia, and then cycle the long way to where Lorna lived and give her a bunch of flowers too. But that would have to wait for another day, I thought, being aware that I'd made a commitment with the boys.

"Come on Kings," they said. "We know that you are Mr. Popular now, and that Lorna Griffiths gets her knickers in a twist just thinking about you. But we have been waiting over an hour for you to come home so we can all go for a bike ride."

"Let's go then Boys," I said, and we all jumped on our bikes and raced down the road towards the village. As we were riding through the village we all rode our bikes in a line, only breaking formation when a car was coming. Jerry seemed quite amused with this new riding arrangement, and he jumped from one bike to the other, landing and riding on our handlebars or shoulders. It was so funny when everytime one of us rode over a bump or jumped over a curb, Jerry flew up into the air, and then landed back on our shoulders or handlebars. He turned it into a game which we played through the village and all the way to Pennard Stores. Jerry was showing more and more of his personality to all of us.

We parked our bikes outside the store and then went inside to buy some refreshers and football cards. Jerry decided to stay on Bryce's shoulder, as he'd been riding on the handlebars of Bryce's bike for the last few minutes of our journey. As soon as Mrs. Ridgley the storekeeper saw Jerry, she ordered Bryce out of the store, so I went in with Jerry on my shoulders. We carried this on for a joke until we had all been kicked out. After Mrs. Ridgley had finished dealing with the last customer in the store, she came outside and responded to our joke.

"You either have four magpies out here, or you are all as stupid as one another, and I would wager it is the latter. You are all quadrupally stupid!"

"Oh, calm down Mrs. Ridgley. We are only teasing you and having a bit of fun!"

"Not today boys, please! I've had a day I'd much rather forget, one awkward customer after the other!"

"Ok, Mrs. Ridgley. Bryce will come in on his own and take our order."

"No, wait boys, don't tell me, let me guess. You want 20 refreshers, that's five each, and 4 packets of football cards, that's one packet each. And I've got nothing for the magpie, so he can stay outside."

"Well done Mrs. Ridgley," we all proclaimed. "You know us well, that is exactly what we wanted to buy!" We sent Bryce in to purchase our order and the rest of us stayed outside with Jerry. As we chewed our refreshers and traded football cards, we counted the days left before we would be on summer holidays.

"We have three weeks to go," Bryce said, having done the math. Eli and I nodded our heads as our mouths were too full of juicy refreshers to speak, and Fraser dribbled out a few words that none of us could understand.

"Gosh these are good!" I finally said, as I swallowed, and then chewed and talked at the same time.

"What did you say?" Bryce mumbled, juice running down his chin. Jerry watched with envy as he took each wrapper into his mouth looking for something to chew on. Fraser was particularly happy with the football cards in his pack. He got two of his favourite Chelsea players, Peter Osgood, and Nicolas Hutchinson, and in between blowing bubbles with his bubble gum, he announced that he wasn't open for trading. The rest of us got players that we already had in our collections, so we would try and trade them at school.

"Jerry is one of the boy's now isn't he," Fraser said. "Now that he's ridden on our bikes with us!"

"Yes he is," we all agreed. "Did you hear that, Jerry?" Eli said. You are one of the gang now, and the five of us made a pact that we would hang out together over the summer holidays. We only had one more Saturday afternoon that we had to work on the Stafford's garden because of the toads. We talked about going fishing for mackerel and bass off the rocks. My Dad had bought an inflatable dinghy that we could take out onto the sea if we wanted to, and there was swimming and surfing and lying in the hot dunes. As the excitement of the summer holidays sank into our minds and hearts, my thoughts went to Olivia's deep brown eyes, and I looked forward to holding hands and kissing, and the way she made me feel. Then there was Lorna Griffiths! What delightful mysteries awaited me there, I pondered, keeping those thoughts to myself.

After finishing our refreshers, and watching Jerry collect all the paper wrappers, Fraser and Eli rode home to Browns Drive, while Jerry and I went back with Bryce to his house, after he assured me that his father, Black Morris would be out. "Come on," he said. "He's out tonight at the pub, and Olivia would love to see you." I hid my bike in a hedge a few houses down from Bryce's place and walked the rest of the way with Jerry tucked inside my jacket just in case Black Morris was unexpectedly home.

When we arrived, I was relieved to see that his car wasn't in the driveway, and Olivia asked her mum if she could go for another walk with me to Pennard Castle. She had finished all her homework, so Mrs. Morris agreed. "Don't be home late you two," she said as we headed out of the door.

"We won't Mrs. Morris, and thank you," I said, feeling excited.

Olivia took my hand, and Jerry rode on my shoulders as we walked through the village and down Bendrick Drive to the golf course. "I was hoping I could see you tonight, Kingsley. I've missed you. It's not the same when the boys are around, and I'm happy we can have this time to ourselves."

"I have missed you too," I replied, and I am excited that we have the summer holidays ahead of us and can spend more time together." Olivia smiled and squeezed my hand as we walked.

"There is something I want to talk to you about, Kingsley."

"What is it?" I replied wondering what she was going to say. I thought maybe she wanted to talk about how awkward things have been with her father not wanting me to come to the house, since the fiasco with Adams and Bullshit Bully, but it wasn't.

"I want to talk to you about Lorna Griffiths," she said. This could be awkward, I thought.

"Yes, what about her?" I asked.

"Well, everyone knows she likes you, Kings, and I don't blame you if you like her too. She is very beautiful with her long blonde hair. I am not jealous. No, that is not entirely true. I am a bit jealous, but not of you! I'm jealous of her because she is so attractive and has the pick of all the boys at school."

"I know she likes Jerry," I replied, not wanting to say more until I knew where the conversation was going.

"Kingsley, this is difficult for me to say, and I hope you don't take it the wrong way, but Lorna Griffiths has got a cold heart, she has only been interested in you since you have become popular with your magpie. She never liked you before, and talked about you behind your back because you are friends with George Matthews, and some of the other boys who live down Sandy Lane. She never took the time to try and get to know you before you had Jerry.

"I know Olivia," I replied, "and I'm not taking what you have said the wrong way. Thank you for caring enough about me to talk to me about her. And it's not just her and the other girls that treat me differently now, it seems everyone does, and I am different now. Since Jerry came into my life I have learned and grown so much as a person, and I think other people see that and treat me differently because of it. I know who my friends were before I became popular, and I know that you have always cared about me Olivia. You took the time to get to know me and be my friend when no one else wanted to, except Bryce and Eli, and of course Fraser, who had no choice because he's my brother. I love you, OLivia, and no one could ever take your place unless you wanted them to."

"I love you too, Kings, and I don't ever want anyone to take my place." We stopped on our walk and hugged and kissed, and I didn't share with her that Lorna Griffiths had rocked my world just by her smile and the conversation I had had with her in the school field. I was changing, that was for sure, because Jerry had taught me to take life as it comes, and to always be myself, which was something I was afraid to do before. Thank you, Jerry Old Boy, for teaching me that life isn't always black and white, sometimes it is green and blue and purple. Olivia is blue, I am green, Lorna Griffiths is purple, and they are all my favourite colours!

Olivia and I arrived at the grounds of Pennard Castle, and its silent storytelling walls spoke loudly, as we listened to the voices upon the wind. "Oh, I love it here, Kings. My soul always feels free standing here before these ancient walls, and I can hear the stories of lovers past, crying out upon the wind."

"It is a most sacred place," I echoed, "and I can hear the voices too, the voices of two hearts that belong to me and you." I took Olivia's hand and led her to the castle room. "Let's sit," I said, putting down my coat upon the sand for her to sit on.

"You are a real gentleman, Kingsley, a true Prince are you!"

"Why thank you my Lady, a true Princess are you!"

As we sat and hugged and kissed, centuries passed, and the walls of Pennard Castle shouted out to us, and told us stories of lovers long ago, and in a hundred years time, our story would be told too, to two more lovers, whose secrets would be kept within these walls. "I love you Kingsley, and I give you my love to hold."

"I love you Olivia, and I give you my love to hold."

After kissing for a hundred years, it seemed it was still not long enough, as Olivia and I came out of our secret room. There on the hill was the stallion we had seen last time we were here, and he was still standing guard over his mare and foal that grazed on the grass of another nearby hill. "He is still here," Olivia said, rather surprised. "I thought he and his family would have left by now."

"No," I replied. "He is still here alright, and he will probably stay until late in the summer when the grazing has gone. Some of the horse families and even the small herds will stay in an area for months on end, as long as they feel safe and are not disturbed by people or dogs. Then they will move somewhere else to find fresh pasture. I have seen a family of horses, including the stallion, stay in the same area until the foal becomes a yearling."

"Wow, you know so much about horses, Kings!"

"They have taught me many things about life and family," I replied, "and especially about how they protect their young. Lessons people should take notice of, and practice within their own families."

We stayed in the castle grounds until sunset, and then climbed one of the highest hills to watch it. "I love it when you take my hand, Kings, and lead me to such special places." I smiled and looked deep into Olivia's brown eyes, that reflected the orange sky out over the bay. The colours were breathtaking! Beautiful reds and purples, and a distant yellow band like a rainbow curved behind the nearer clouds to the west.

TWILIGHT STILL

There is a time before the darkness,
But it is after the days bright
When my soul stands still.
TWILIGHT STILL

The Sun, she lays down her head
still glowing through her blankets
upon the western sky.
She is still before she dreams in the shadows
TWILIGHT STILL

The sleeping hours of the day
have been lived and have gone
and they still live in my memories song.
TWILIGHT STILL

The night clouds they come wearing
Their silent silver gown and
the skylark is quiet below.
I watch as the moon races
the silence over the hill.
It is then that my soul knows
it is Twilight still,
TWILIGHT STILL, TWILIGHT STILL

After the most brilliant of the colours faded, we waited and watched as the night clouds told us stories of the day's happy hours, and for Olivia and I, this sunset was ours.

We arrived back at Olivia's house, just as the last of the lights said goodnight, and we said goodbye on the porch because Black Morris's car was in the driveway. "Goodnight Kings, thank you for a lovely evening, sweet dreams until we meet again."

"Sweet dreams my brown eyed girl, until we meet again."

Chapter Twelve

Sports Day!

The remainder of the school term before the summer holidays was the most dear to me in all my school years that I can remember. These days and weeks that I had Jerry and discovered who Kingsley Hill 'really was' was a wonderful time! To have the chance to learn and grow on an even playing field with everyone else, not beaten and bullied, and spending long hours in fear was so wonderfully liberating. This wonderful season in my life did not heal my deepest wounds from bullies and asthma, but it taught me how to start my journey in rising above them, and forming scars over those wounds so that they could one day heal.

Jerry, who now didn't need to be closed in his cage at night anymore, slept on the headboard of my bed. My mother came into my room and caught him several times, and ordered him outside, but we soon had a good routine worked out. When I heard mother coming up the stairs, I quickly opened my bedroom window and Jerry flew out! He may not have been able to speak in human language, but he sure knew when to make himself scarce. Once Jerry had flown out of the window and had been gone for 10 minutes, I stood at the window and opened it again, and back in he would fly! On several occasions he saw my mother still in the bedroom talking to me after he had been gone for 10 minutes, and then he made a reconnaissance flight back and forth in front of the window and disappeared again for another 10 minutes. He then tapped on the window to see if it was all clear. "You smart bird," I said, and gave him half of my sandwich.

Each school day afternoon, Jerry would arrive at the school within minutes of 3:45, just before the end of school, bell rang. Then he would knock on my classroom window wanting to play soccer with us boys, or sometimes he would sit on the girls shoulders while they skipped over their skipping ropes and sang songs. I often listened to the songs the girls made up about Jerry as they skipped and jumped in unison over their ropes, and I listened even more carefully to the songs they made up about us boys, and I would often hear my name. At lunch times Jerry played Marbles with the boys, and Jacks with the girls, and even played Hopscotch, by moving the stones that the girls threw onto the various squares.

Jerry became the school yard hero, showing us all the perfect example of friendship and acceptance. Whether you lived in Sandy Lane or came from a Middle or Upper class family, he broke all the barriers down! Jerry was the friend of the friendless, and the biggest advocate for anti-bullying there was. He lived by example, and taught us all to love deeper. He never criticised or judged, and I'm sure that being given half a sandwich and some cheese puffs were the only bribes he accepted.

On Sports Day, our last day of school before the Summer Holidays, Jerry stole Mr. Richards shiny sports whistle, and I didn't even get in trouble. I assumed he had another one as Jerry flew around the sports field with it and wouldn't give it back.

Sports days had all too often been a sad day for me, as I was either home sick with an asthma attack or getting over one and unable to compete. And last year I was threatened by Jeff Adams and his gang to not compete, otherwise I would be beaten up! I remember that sports day well. I watched from the crowd as Adams took first place in the 100 metre Sprint. I listened to the crowd shouting and cheering as he passed the finish line, knowing that it could have been me. I was the fastest runner in the school, not Adams. He gave me a cruel look as Mr. Emlyn the headmaster presented him with the revered trophy and then pinned a medal on his shirt. Mervin Howell won the 200 metre race last year, which I also could have won, and my heart sank as the cheers and shouts filled the air.

Today however was my turn! Adams was still too bandaged up and broken to compete this year. Andrew Bowen was my nearest rival in the 100 metre today. Howell was running in the 200 and hoping to retain his crown which he won last year when I was home sick with asthma. I was running in the 200 metre today too, and I looked forward to challenging him for his crown.

Before the running events, Fraser, Eli and I walked around the sports field watching some of the other competitions. Bryce competed in the High Jump and came in 2nd, and also my friend George Matthews from Sandy Lane was competing in the Long Jump, and he came in fourth. I felt sorry for George because his mother and father never once came to a sports day to watch him, not that many of us kids wanted our parents around, but when neither one of them shows up, you don't feel very important. One year George Matthews came in 2nd in the Long Jump, and received a medal from Mr. Richards, and I watched as he looked around for some acknowledgement for his achievement, and the only sound he heard was booing and laughing from Adams and his thugs. But back to the present day!

Finally Mr. Emlyn's voice came over the loudspeaker, and said, "Ladies and Gentlemen, Boys and Girls, it's time for the event that we have all been waiting for! The 100 metre Sprint which will determine the fastest runner in the school." As all the competitors made their way to the starting line, I felt nervous as well as excited, and my heart was beating fast.

As we all got in line, Mr. Emlyn also reminded everyone on the field, how the various House Points were standing. Each person who attended Pennard School was assigned to one of four different houses. The houses were named after local birds here on the Gower Peninsula. For example, Fraser belonged to Seagull House, Eli to Swallow House, Bryce was in Robin House, and I was assigned to the Linnets. At the end of Sports Day, all the points were added up from all four houses, and the winners were announced in order of how many points were achieved by their prospective athletes, coming in 1st, 2nd, 3rd, or 4th. So as well as individual achievements, there were house team achievements too. Adams was in Swallow House, and anyone who wasn't a Swallow was a loser in his books, apart from Howell and Bowen who were both Robins, so if you were a Seagull or a Linnet, you were despised by the bullies.

As we took our places at the starting line, it was as if time stood still for a few minutes as I glanced all around me. Jerry sat on Fraser's shoulder as Fraser stood on the left side of the starting line next to my mother who had come with her friend Joan Hall. Several other parents stood on each side of the starting line, including Eli's sister Debbie. Towards the end of the 100 metre track, parents and children now stood shoulder to shoulder, and elbow to elbow, wanting to be as close to the finishing line as they could, and my heart now started to pound!

"You can do it," I said to myself, in defiance of the voices that said I couldn't, and Mr. Emlyn, the Headmaster, lifted the red and white starting flag into the air.

A great hush seemed to come over the whole sports-field, and everything seemed to be in slow motion, as I heard the words, "On your marks, Get ready, Go!"

Off I went, powering away with all my heart, and it was as if I was leaving behind me with every stride I took towards the finish line, every punch, every kick, every word of ridicule that Adams and all his cronies had ever said to me. I ran fast and straight, and kept looking straight ahead towards the finish line. It seemed that we were no longer in this bubble of slow motion, and I could feel my heart pumping inside my body, and my muscles pushing my legs as fast as they would carry me. I kept my arms moving back and forth at my side, and tried to control my breathing as I could see the finish line in the distance. I could hear the cheers and shouts now as I got closer and closer, and the muscles in my legs began to burn! I was tempted to look behind me because I sensed I was ahead, but I kept looking straight ahead. There was no one in my peripheral vision to my left or to my right, but suddenly I felt something land on my shoulder and then take off again. It was Jerry! And he now flew in front of me as if leading the way. He reached the finish line, and then flew high into the air, and people shouted and cheered as seconds later down came the chequered flag, and I crossed the finish line! Now I slowed and looked back, and everyone else was still behind me! I've won! I've won! I thought, as about six people jumped on top of me in celebration of my win.

"You did it! You did it!" Bryce and Eli shouted. "Well done Kings, you are the fastest runner in the school!" A shadow appeared now above us, and it was Jerry coming in for a landing, and he landed right on my head, as if crowning me the **100** meters King!

"Your magpie led the way, Kings," a girl shouted from the crowd. "Did you follow him to the finish line, Kings?"

"Yes," I replied. "I followed him all the way!"

"It will soon be time to start the **200** metre race," Mr. Emlyn announced over the loudspeaker. "Can all competitors take their places at the starting line." As I arrived at the starting line, Lorna Griffiths came up to me and wished me well with her pretty smile and lipstick.

"Olivia is not well today," Bryce had said, and was home from school sick.That's why I haven't seen her, I pondered. I had wondered why she hadn't been at the **100** meter finish line. What a day to get sick, I thought. I knew that feeling well, and I would try and win another medal for her today. Eli was also running in the **200** metre, and Fraser and Briyce were cheering us on.

Sports Day was already all I could have hoped it would be, a day to remember. No, it was far more than that, it was a day that I would never forget! Not only had I won the **100** metre sprint and was crowned the fastest runner in the school, but I also won the **200** metre race! Mervin Howell came in fuming behind me. I guess he was upset because he couldn't retain his title. Eli came in third and took the bronze medal.

Mr. Richards came over to congratulate me, and said I was so far ahead in the **100** metre sprint that I was **30** feet in front of Bowen who came in 2nd. And I even got to compete in the **300** metre race, only I was tired from the first two races, but I still finished in 3rd place.

What a wonderful day. I didn't want it to end. And as I held up the revered 100 metre trophy and my medals for the school photographs, all my friends shouted, "Well done Kings," and Lorna Griffiths had made a daisy chain and put it around my neck and kissed me. Even if what Olivia said was true, and she did only like me because I was popular and had Jerry as my pet, it sure felt good to be kissed by the most beautiful girl in the school!

In the evening Jerry brought Mr. Richards's shiny sports whistle to my bedroom window, and I kept it as a momentum to go with my trophy and medals for winning the races. "Thank you Old Boy, is that my trophy from you? I love you boy, and I am so glad that you were with me today. We did it together, didn't we?" Jerry flew up and down, and then hopped around me as if he understood exactly what I said. I'm sure he did.

Chapter Thirteen

A Black and White Pirate

It felt strange, wonderfully strange, to wake up on Monday morning and not have school. What was I going to do today, I thought as I stretched and looked up at the headboard of my bed. Jerry was perched quietly on top of the headboard with his eyes closed, and he was making a low pitched squeaking noise as he breathed. Maybe it was the equivalent of a human snore. It was a rare thing to see him sleeping, and he looked like he didn't have a care in the world. As I watched him, I felt my love for him in my heart. Before I met Jerry, I didn't think that I could love a bird. Like one, yes, but it was only dogs and cats, and horses that people loved, I thought. Jerry had proved me wrong, and I couldn't imagine being without him now.

On Wednesday afternoon, it was Nicolas Hall's birthday party. Nicolas lived next door, and because his mother Joan was my mum's best friend. Fraser and I were invited to his birthday party. Of course his younger sister Pauline would be there too. Pauline's birthday had only been a month previous, and Mr. and Mrs. Hall had given her a silver necklace with several precious stones in it. "Sapphires, I think," so Mrs. Hall had said.

Fraser had already gone over to the party, while I had been feeding Jerry his lunch of garden worms, and

173

some warm milk, which was his favorite meal when we were at home and not looking for sandhoppers down on the beach. "Come on Jerry," I said, as he finished his last worm. "It's time that we crashed the party next door." Nicolas was more Fraser's friend, and he wasn't particularly fond of Bryce and Eli who hadn't been invited. "Oh, well, you and I can hang out, Old Boy," I said as I opened the garden gate with Jerry perched on my shoulder.

Jerry of course joined in the fun immediately, playing games with the guests. He chased balloons, and landed on peoples shoulders. A few of the girls were scared of him, as he landed on their heads and tried to pull the ribbons from their hair. "You sure like bright and shiny things, don't you Old Boy. Now you behave! Not everyone has seen a tame magpie, and is used to a bird landing on their heads."

As Fraser hung out with Nicolas, and my mum helped Aunty Joan with the food and party games, I began to feel bored and out of place. Nicolas was almost two years younger than me, and a year younger than Fraser, so he wasn't in the same class as either of us at school, and I didn't know any of his friends. I'll wait until I have a piece of birthday cake, I thought, and then slip away with Jerry. I watched as Nicolas opened his birthday presents, and then Aunty Joan announced that it was time for the birthday cake. Mr. Hall arrived carrying the cake, and began to sing Happy Birthday and we all joined in. Jerry was having a hayday with the wrapping paper from the presents, as I sat down with Nicolas's sister Pauline and her friend at the picnic table. I wolfed down a large piece of birthday cake. "I like your necklace," I said to Pauline, having thought of something to say.

"Would you like to have a look at it, Kings? It was my special present that I got for my birthday!" Before I could say anything, Pauline unclipped it from her neck, and handed it to me to have a look at. It was then that it happened!

Jerry, who had finished playing with the wrapping paper, swooped down from a tree and snatched the necklace from my hand! Pauline and her friend screamed, while Jerry, who had taken to the air, carried the necklace over the hedge and into Downes Field. "Mum!" Pauline cried, "Jerry the Magpie has stolen my necklace!"

Both Mum and Mrs. Hall came running over to the picnic table, and asked what had happened. "He came from nowhere," I explained. "Jerry was playing with the wrapping paper from the presents, then next thing I know, he swooped down from the tree and snatched Pauline's necklace!"

"Oh, Kingsley!" My mother said, with a look of disdain. "How could you let Jerry steal Pauline's necklace?"

"I didn't let him, Mum, he just swooped down and took it!"

"What were you doing taking it off your neck, Pauline?" Mrs. Hall said, in a scolding tone of voice.

"I wanted to show Kingsley," Pauline replied, bursting into tears. Mr. Hall arrived on the scene now, and reminded us that it was a very expensive Silver necklace with Sapphires.

"And where is Jerry now?" he asked, looking right at me, and I pointed over to Downes Field.

"You will have to get it back Kingsley," Mrs. Hall said. "That necklace was Pauline's special birthday present!"

"Right away, Aunty Joan," I replied. "I will go and find Jerry right now," and I climbed over the hedge and into Downes Field.

As I walked through the field keeping my eyes peeled to the ground, Jerry and the necklace were nowhere to be seen. I spent an hour looking for the necklace in the grass, although I doubted that Jerry would have dropped it. He would more likely be playing with it somewhere. "Jerry! Jerry!" I called. "Bring that necklace back now!" I walked to the far end of the field where Bullshit Bully used to stand underneath the big oak tree, but still there was no sign of Jerry or the necklace anywhere. He must have gone on one of his longer flights, I thought. Now that he was almost an adult, he was flying further distances.

By the time I had climbed back over the hedge to the party, most of the guests had left, and my Mum was sitting with Mr. and Mrs. Hall at the picnic table waiting for me to get back.

"Well?" my mother said. "Where is Pauline's necklace?"

"I don't know, Mum," I replied. "I have looked everywhere and there is no sign of Jerry or the necklace. Mr. Hall looked at me and shook his head, and then went inside his house.

"I don't know what to say, Joy," Aunty Joan said to my mother. "Please encourage Kingsley to keep looking for it."

I answered for my mother, and said, "I won't stop looking until I find it, Aunty Joan, and I am so sorry!"

"Please keep looking for it, Kingsley," she replied a final time sounding disappointed, and then disappeared into the house leaving me at the picnic table with Mum.

"You better pray that Jerry doesn't lose that necklace, Kingsley," she said, "or you will have to pay for it."

"Yeah, yeah, I get it!" I replied feeling frustrated. "What else do you want me to do? We will have to wait until Jerry gets back, and hopefully he will have it in his beak." As I stared back at the house, I saw Pauline's face looking out of her bedroom window, and she was still crying.

She opened the window and shouted, "I hate your magpie, Kingsley! Jerry has turned into a Pirate!"

"Yeah, he's no better than Long John Silver," Fraser joked, leaning over the garden fence.

"You mean Long John Jerry," Pauline shouted from her window having heard what Fraser had said, and I began to laugh.

"This is not funny," Mum scolded, "and if you can't find the necklace, Kingsley, you will have to pay for it with your pocket money!" Well, that was the worst party that I have been to, I thought, as Mum headed back into our house.

"Do you think Jerry will bring it back, Kings?" Fraser asked, still leaning over the fence from our garden.

"I don't know," I replied. "I don't think he would have dropped it. He's probably stashed it somewhere with all his other shiny treasures," and I waited at the Hall's picnic table for Jerry to return. This was the longest time he had ever stayed away, I thought as I walked back to my house, and I waited in the back garden and stared across the field, awaiting his return. The minutes went by and then the hours and still he did not come, and I wondered if something had happened to him. I didn't much care if I got the necklace back now, I just wanted him to come home.

Finally, just before dark, I could see in the distance a black and white bird bobbing over the hedgerows and flying across Downes Field. "It has to be him," I spoke aloud, and my heart began to beat faster. "Jerry! Jerry!" I shouted. I could see now that it was him, and he flew right over the back hedge and then landed on my shoulder. "Where have you been, Old Boy," I said. "I have been so worried. I am so glad that you're back." He jumped up onto my head and started pecking my ear. "It's good to see you too, Old Boy, but we are in deep shit! Where is Pauline's necklace, Old Boy? What have you done with it? If we don't get it back I will have to pay for it out of my pocket money, and it's very expensive! If you don't bring it back, there are no more refreshers or football cards, and no Cornish pasties for you Old Boy." Jerry continued to play with my hair and nibble at my ears, until it was time to call it a night. "You know the routine," I said. "You stay out here in the back garden until I open the bedroom window and then you can come in. And remember, if you see Mum in the bedroom, don't fly in until she has gone. She is not in a good mood tonight, and won't take too kindly to you sleeping in my room, Long John Jerry. Everyone thinks you're a necklace stealing pirate Old Boy!" And he was.

Before Jerry and I fell asleep for the night, Fraser said that he would help me look for the necklace in the morning when we got up. "At Least there is no school tomorrow, Kings," he said, "so we can spend the whole day looking if we have to."

"Thanks Fraser," I replied, but it was going to be like looking for a needle in a haystack I thought, and I was already grieving the loss of my pocket money, especially now that we were on our summer holidays. I needed money to spend on Olivia, and Lorna too. Jerry sat on the headboard of my bed as usual and we both drifted off to sleep.

It was Thursday morning, and after breakfast, Fraser and I dug some worms for Jerry in the garden, and then headed off with Jerry to see if he would lead us to the necklace. "Come on Old Boy," I said. "If you lead us to the necklace, I will give you a whole Cornish pasty for yourself," but as we walked across Downes Field, Jerry seemed more interested in playing than earning himself a pasty.

"I wonder where he has stashed it," Fraser said, as we reached the end of the field.

"I don't think it's on the ground," I replied. "Magpies like to collect things and hide them in secret places, or not so secret places."

"What do you mean, not so secret places?" Fraser asked.

"Well, what if he has hidden it right in front of our noses? Or somewhere so obvious that we wouldn't even think of looking there!"

"Like an old magpie's nest or something," Fraser replied.

"Yes exactly! Somewhere that would be out of reach and secret, but close by. Wait a minute, Fraser," I said. "At the far end of the field where Bullshit Bully used to stand under the big oak, there is an old magpie's nest in the hawthorne thicket. It's just before the wooden gate into the next field. I remember Eli and I found it one year when we were collecting bird eggs. It's worth a try. Come on Jerry," I said. "Can you show us where you put Pauline's necklace?" As we approached the hawthorn thicket, Jerry flew back and forth between Fraser and I , landing on our shoulders and wanting to play. "Come on Old Boy," I said feeling frustrated. "This may be a game for you, but I'm in trouble here, and I need our help!"

Just as I finished speaking, Jerry, who had landed on my shoulder, took to the air and flew in front of us across the field. "He is leading us somewhere!" Fraser exclaimed, and we watched him fly to the far end of the field and land on the wooden gate. Fraser and I ran now to catch him up, and arrived at the gate.

"There is the nest in the thicket," I pointed out to Fraser.

"Look at all the stick roofs over the nest," he said.

"Yes," I replied. "A magpie will often use the same nest for years, if they are not desturbed, and will build a new roof over the nest each year."

Fraser counted the roofs, and said, "there are seven of them, one on top of the other." In the middle of our conversation, Jerry flew up into the thicket, and perched just above the nest. "He's leading us to the nest," Fraser said excitedly.

"I think you're right," I replied. "Now one of us has to climb up into the thicket and check the nest." Hawthorn trees have lovely smelling pink and white blossoms in the spring, but their thorns can pierce and tear your skin apart in seconds when trying to climb them.

"I'm not climbing up there, Kings," my brother said adamantly. "And besides I've got my new jeans on, and Mum will go ballistic if I hole these!"

"I don't fancy getting torn up either," I replied, "but I will climb up and check the nest. Is this where Pauline's necklace is, Old Boy?" I said to Jerry as I started to climb the thicket. I hope so, because I'm going to get torn to pieces climbing up here! "Gosh this is a thick tree," I called out, "more like a thorn bush, ahhh!" I shouted. I soon had cuts and scratches on my arms and legs as the thorns pierced through my clothing, but I kept going, breaking off branches and thorns as I climbed. Finally I reached the top of the tree. Jerry remained on a branch above the nest and watched while I anticipated putting my hand into the nest to see what was inside.

"Can you reach the nest?" Fraser called from below.

"I think so," I replied, "but there is a thick roof of twigs right over it, and the entrance to the nest must be on the other side." I began to pull the sticks away. "I wish I had some gloves," I said, as I began to feel around the side of the nest for the entrance. "There must be an entrance big enough for the magpie to get in somewhere!" I shouted. Suddenly I pushed my thumb right onto a sharp thorn. "Damn it!" I yelled loudly, pulling my hand back and licking my wound. The thorn had gone deep into my thumb, and it throbbed with pain.

"What's the matter?" Fraser called up. "Have you found the entrance yet?"

"No," I replied. "I just punctured my thumb against a big thorn." Not finding the entrance into the nest, I began pulling away at the sticks and thorns with my other hand, until finally there was enough room for me to get my hand inside. I put my hand into the nest and felt around the sides. It was lined with grass and hair, and I couldn't reach the bottom of the nest without readjusting my position in the tree. I pushed my way through some more thorns and branches to get even closer, and then pushed my hand to the bottom of the nest. Instantly I became excited as I felt coins and other objects at the bottom of the nest. "There is something in here!" I shouted down to Fraser.

"What is it?" he called back excitedly.

"I think there's coins," I said as I gripped them with my fingers and slowly lifted them out of the nest. There were five 50 pence pieces! "Wow, this is a goldmine,"I said to Jerry. I only get 50 pence a week pocket money, and I've got five weeks worth here. Jerry continued to sit on his perch above me, quite undaunted at my find."Thank you Boy, this will do very nicely, thank you very much!" I put the coins in my pocket, and then reached into the bottom of the nest again. This time I could feel what felt like two metal objects, and I pulled one out at a time, fearing I would drop one if I tried to lift them both out at the same time.

The first item was cold and heavy, and felt like a watch. I could feel it had a metal band as I lifted it up the side of the nest,and out through the hole I'd made. I then put it into my other hand to inspect it as I tried to maintain my balance in the tree. "What is it?" Fraser shouted. I was too engulfed in what I was doing to answer him, and I could see that it was a beautiful old watch. It looked to be made of Silver, and it was still working. I could see the hands on the watch were moving. Slowly, I lowered it to my side and pushed it into my pocket, and I felt my body weight starting to shift in the tree. "Are you alright, Kings?" I heard Fraser anxiously questioning.

"Yes," I replied. "I'm just trying to keep my balance in the tree." I then tried to reposition myself, so I could put my hand into the nest again. This time I felt all around the sides of the nest. I didn't want to miss anything. There wasn't anything stuck in the sides of the nest, no necklace or anything else that I could feel, so I lowered my hand into the bottom of the nest again, and felt the other metal object. This was cool to my touch too, and was obviously metal, and it felt round and heavy. Slowly I pulled it through the hole in the nest and held it up closely to inspect it. My gosh it was a beautiful bracelet, gold in colour, and had the initials J.G. imprinted on the front.

I turned it over to look at the back, and there were more words inscripted on it. It read, 'To my darling Jonathan on the occasion of our first wedding anniversary, from your loving wife Avril'. Wow! "I'm coming down now," I said to Fraser, and I started making my way down through the thorns. "I hope you didn't steal all these things, Jerry," I said, as he left his perch and flew back and forth from the bottom of the thicket where Fraser was standing to where I was in the tree. "Actually, I'm glad if you did take them Jerry," I said, as he joined me now in the tree. "Easy for you, Old Boy," I said. "You can just fly down the tree, but I have to get through all these thorns!" I finally reached the bottom of the tree, and I had more cuts and tears on my clothes than I could shake a stick at, so to speak, and my thumb was still throbbing.

"What did you find, Kings?" Fraser said in anticipation, and I emptied my pockets of the five 50 pence pieces, and the watch, but I kept the bracelet secretly in my other pocket. "Wow, Kings, you found a goldmine! Are you going to share some with me? It was partly my idea to look in the magpie's nest."

"Of course I'm going to share with you, who do you think I am, Jeff Adams or something? I'm going to give you two of the 50 pence pieces, and we can split whatever we get for the watch."

"Thanks Kings! This is amazing!"

"Yeah, it isn't it, we found a stash alright, and this has given me another idea!"

"What is it, Kings?"

Well, just suppose that this isn't Jerry's stash, and it belongs to another magpie."

"Then Jerry must still have his stash somewhere," Fraser said, catching my drift.

"Exactly," I replied, "and it is quite likely that he has put Pauline's necklace in a magpie's nest, even if it's not his own nest, it is made by one of his species, and is a perfect place to hide something."

"Plus we might find other treasures in other nests," Fraser continued.

"Yes," I replied, getting more excited. "I think we should search all the magpie nests that we can find, and we'll make a fortune! But I need you to help me, Fraser, I can't do all the climbs myself. I'm cut to pieces, look at me!"

"Ok, I'll do some climbs too, Kings, as long as we share the profits."

"So let's shake on it," I said, "and then we have a deal." We shook hands.

As we made our way home across the field, we decided to give Jerry a full "Pirate Status" for guiding us to find the loot! "Did you hear that Old Boy, you're Long John Jerry now, a full partner in crime. You just keep collecting the coins Old Boy, and we will make a fortune, and for every 5 pounds you collect, we will buy you a whole Cornish pasty." We also decided not to tell Bryce or Eli about our find, so that we could check all the magpie nests without anyone else sharing the profits.

When we arrived back at the house, Mum was anxious to know whether we had found the necklace. "No Mum," I replied, "but we did spend a long time looking for it. I even climbed a hawthorn tree to look inside a magpie's nest, in case Jerry had put it in there."

"Yeah, we looked really hard Mum", Fraser said, backing me up. "We will just have to hope that Jerry brings the necklace back."

"You better hope he does," Mum replied, "because I meant what I said. There is no more pocket money for you Kingsley, until it's paid for, or Jerry brings it back!"

Mum then scolded me for the tears in my clothes, and said I needed to wash the blood off my hands and put a bandage on before I sat down for lunch. "How on earth did you get in such a state?" she cussed.

"I told you Mum, I climbed a hawthorn tree to see if the necklace was in a magpie's nest."

Chapter Fourteen

Go Blow Your Yoke

The first week of the summer holidays, Fraser, Bryce, Eli and I, had spent most of our time riding our bikes. We visited all our favourite haunts, including Broad Pool, where we had got the toads earlier in the spring. The toads had almost all gone now, which was a good thing, because Eli and I had added a few more people to our mailing list. Broad Pool was now full of tadpoles, and baby frogs that were just losing their tails in order to start their adventures on land. "Being an amphibian has many advantages," Bryce said, picking up a small frog. "You can live in water or on land."

Jerry continued to join us on our adventures, and ate 10 baby frogs one morning while they were trying to leave the pond to start their lives on land.

"That was a brief life they had," Fraser said, as Jerry tore them apart and gulped them down.

"They must taste like refreshers to magpies," Bryce said.

"Rather he ate them than me," I replied. "I still prefer my refreshers with the wrapping paper on and not hopping across the grass," and everybody laughed.

It was during the second week of the holidays that I noticed a change in Jerry. He began to spend less time with us, and was often gone for four or five hours at a time. He was obviously up to something mischievous, but what? "Maybe he's restocking the old nest with new coins," Fraser whispered, so that Bryce and Eli didn't hear.

"I hope so," I whispered back. "I want to buy some more football cards, and I don't have any pocket money coming in now until the necklace is paid for." Not that I was short of money. I still had my stash from the magpie's nest, and also money coming in every week from my milkround with Eli's brother Philip, and I had an old silver watch and a special bracelet to sell when I wanted to. I was saving up to buy some special things for Olivia and Lorna Griffiths, and I was sure looking forward to spending some more time with them.

"We will go and check the nest again tonight Fraser," I said.

"Sounds good," he replied with a smile.

As soon as Bryce and Eli headed home for the evening, Fraser and I made our way across Downes Field to the nest. To our surprise, Jerry was already at the top of the field, and he was with another magpie! "So this is who you have been spending your time with, Old Boy," I said, "and what's your friend's name? I'm sure it must be Maggie," I answered for Jerry, and he fluttered up and down as if to say 'yes, her name is Maggie'!

"I wonder if it is a girl?" Fraser said.

"Oh, I'm sure it is," I replied, "and maybe they have a nest."

"Do you think they are going to have babies, Kings?"

"I don't know," I replied. "I didn't think that Jerry was old enough to mate yet, but if they have built a nest together, maybe he is." Just then both Jerry and the other magpie flew out of the thicket and started flying across the neighbouring field. "Let's follow them," I said. "It is unlikely that they have collected that many more treasures in this nest since last week. Let's see if they are leading us to another nest."

Fraser had his heart set on us checking this nest again, after the treasures I had had found in it already, but he reluctantly agreed to follow the magpies with me across the next field, to see where they led us.

At the far end of the next field there was another nest, and Jerry and Maggie were cackling around the thicket, and landing on the branches just above the nest. "I think it's Jerry's nest," Fraser said, rubbing his hands in excitement, "and I bet they have a stash of coins in there! They are making more of a fuss about this nest than the other one."

"They are," I replied, getting as excited as Fraser was.

"How about I make the climb this time, Kings?" Fraser said, his eyes as big as saucers.

"Yes," I replied, looking at my thumb. "I'm still healing from my cuts and splinters from last time."

"Is it that bad, Kings?" Fraser asked.

"Yes," I replied. "Those thorns are really painful when they break your skin."

Fraser shouted and cursed as he made his way up the tree, and the other magpie seemed quite annoyed as Fraser got closer to the nest. I could sure see which one was the wild magpie, I thought. Jerry isn't making a fuss at all. I know that crows will actually dive bomb you if you get close to their nests. I've had that happen on several occasions while collecting their eggs. Fraser continued to shout and swear as he got caught in the thorns and tried to get free.

"You have to break them off with your hands," I shouted up the tree, but I don't think he heard me.

"I hope this is worth it," he shouted down.

"Me too," I shouted back. Finally the shouting and cursing stopped, and he appeared to be at the top of the tree. I walked back away from the thicket to get a better view from the field.

"I'm right at the top now, Kings!" he shouted down. And then there was silence for what seemed like a long time. What is he doing? I thought. I hope he isn't stuffing any treasures into a secret pocket like I did, I pondered, feeling my pirate greed.

Finally the silence was broken, and shouts of jubilation filled the evening air. "Bloody heck, Kings, there are loads of coins in here! What's this? Kings, there's a ring! He's knicked someone's ring! It looks like gold too, Kings, and there are about 10 coins!"

"How much?" I shouted, feeling tempted to start climbing up the tree myself.

"There are four 50 pence pieces, six 10 pence pieces, four shillings, and three tanners! I'm rich! I'm bloody well rich!" Fraser shouted from the top of the tree, and I danced around in excitement and sang a song.

LONG JOHN JERRY MAGPIE, IS A FRIEND OF MINE

Long John Jerry Magpie, he is a friend of mine
He goes in people's pockets, and their coins go
chime chime chime!

Jerry the Magpie

Long John Jerry Magpie, he is a friend of mine.
He is partial to silver watches,
and gold bracelets all the time,
if you don't have a fifty pence piece,
a ten penny one will do,
and if you don't have one of them, then God bless you!

No cheap stuff for my magpie,
only the most expensive will do
Steal me a nice gold ring, Jerry, I don't mind if you do
And some more fifty pence pieces,
and I'll share my Pasty with you!

Long John Jerry Magpie, I'm very fond of you,
so steal me some
earrings or a pocket watch will do.
Come on Jerry Magpie I'll share the profits with you..

You love to steal necklaces, and crash people's parties too
And I don't know why people get so mad with you,
because
I want to be just like you.

Jerry is a Welshman and Jerry is a thief,
he stole Pauline's
necklace and the old man's false teeth, and then he came
to my house and stole my mothers beef.
Long John
Jerry Magpie you are a bloody thief!

Fraser laughed and cursed all the way down the tree, and then he claimed this place as his territory by pulling it out and going pee. As soon as Fraser had licked his wounds from the thorns, we counted out the loot. "There are two pounds and 80 pence, all in, Kings, and one gold ring! Three French Hens, Two Turtle Doves, and a Magpie in a Hawthorn Tree!" We both sang and laughed.

"That is one pound and 40 pence each, Kings," Fraser said, handing me my cut, "and we can sell the ring and split it. It's gold I'm sure of it," he said, biting it with his teeth.

"Let's have a look," I said, and I rolled it in my fingers.

"Let's take it to one of the jewelers in Swansea on Saturday," Fraser said.

"A good idea," I replied. "How about we take the bus into town after I finish my milkround."

"Yeah, ok Kings."

As we walked home across the fields, we came to the conclusion that other magpies were also collecting coins and treasures, and that was why we had found so much stuff in only two nests. "This is how we are going to make a fortune, Fraser," I said, with a continuous smile on my face, but as we climbed over the hedge to the house, my smile was soon wiped off my face. There, parking in our driveway was 'Die Book and Pencil', our local constabulary.

"Hello Kingsley and Fraser," he said, getting out of his car. "I need to talk to you, Kingsley, with your mother."

"Shit! What does he want," I said under my breath.

"He wants to see you, Kings." Fraser said lifting his eyebrows.

"Yeah, tell me about it, Fraser, what's new!"

"It is about your magpie, Kingsley," Die Book said, and he rang the doorbell. "Hello Mr. and Mrs. Hill," he said. "We need to sit down and have a talk with Kingsley."

"What's going on?" my father asked. We all sat down at the kitchen table except Fraser who was excused to the living room.

"There have been a lot of complaints about Kingsley's magpie," Die Book said, "and something has to be done about it."

"What sort of complaints?" my mother asked. I sat quietly thinking about the events of the last few weeks. Apart from Jerry stealing Pauline's necklace, I couldn't think of any other trouble Jerry had been in. Mom put some tea on and I listened to the accusations.

"I am sorry to bother you Mr. and Mrs. Hill, but as I said, I've had several complaints about Kingsley's magpie from concerned people in the village. First of all, he is landing on ladies heads and pecking at their earrings." I pinched myself underneath the table, trying not to smile, as Die Book continued his case against the accused. "One lady had just come out from getting her hair done, and your magpie landed on her perm and stole one of her earrings, pure silver it was too, she said." Mom and Dad looked at me, and I pinched myself harder, trying not to laugh. "And then there is the milk money, Kingsley," he said looking in my direction. "He's stealing the money that people are leaving out to pay the milkman for their milk, Mr. and Mrs. Hill."

"What? Kingsley's stealing the money?" My mother asked.

"No, Jerry is Mum," I spoke up. "Not me!" I could see that Dad was trying to compose himself now, and trying not to laugh, and I pinched myself harder.

"And if that wasn't enough, Mr. and Mrs. Hill, Jerry flew into Pennard Stores on Wednesday, and frightened Mrs. Ridgley and her customers. He even stole some fresh meat right off the counter that Mrs. Ridgley had just cut for a customer. What do you have to say about all this then, Kingsley?"

"I don't have anything to say about it, Sergeant Jones Sir," I replied.

"You better have something to say about it boy, otherwise we will have to capture your magpie and take him away somewhere where he can't bother people." I was silent as I pondered Die Books words.

"Take him away?!" I spoke aloud. "I can't have him taken away, Dad!"

There was silence around the table for a minute as reality sunk in. Die Book finally broke the silence. "I'd like to make a suggestion to Kingsley and to you Mr. and Mrs. Hill. I would like you to consider putting Jerry into the Penscynor Wildlife Park, where he won't get into trouble. You can still visit him there, Kingsley, and people can enjoy him and he won't be a menace to the community. Things will only get worse unless you keep him caged all the time."

"He needs to be wild and free," I shouted out, not locked up in a cage, or taken to a bird garden!" I ran up to my bedroom not wanting to hear more..

"I heard it all, Kings," Fraser said, following me upstairs to the bedroom, and he sat with me until Die Book and Pencil had left.

Dad then called up to Fraser and I to come down stairs. "You heard what the policeman said, Kings. Something has to be done right away."

"I'm not giving him up Dad, to go to some bird gardens or zoo where he will be caged up like some domestic budgie. He's wild and needs to be free!"

"The problem is, Kings, he's only half wild, and only half tame! This is what I feared would happen, Old Son. Jerry doesn't have any fear of people, or very little of it. The other magpie doesn't land on peoples heads and steal their jewelry, does he? Or sit on your shoulders while you're riding your bike. This is the down side about having a wild magpie as your pet, Kings."

"Ok Dad. I get the message alright!" I responded angrily.

"Now Kings, listen to me. I want to save you a lot of heartache and pain down the road by helping you to make a wise decision now. You can take him to the bird gardens and know that he is safe, and you can visit him whenever you like, or have something bad happen to him in the near future. It seems obvious to me that there is only one wise choice, Kings. It's your choice, Old son, but Jerry can't go on frightening people, and stealing things."

"No! I'm not giving him up Dad, he is my magpie and no one else's."

"Nobody is questioning who Jerry belongs to, it's just very important that you make the right decision in doing what is best for him. Otherwise something is likely to happen that you will later regret."

"And as I said, Dad, I'm not ready to give him up!"

We talked for a few minutes more, trying to come up with another solution. Finally, Dad sighed and said, "Then this is what I would do Kings, if I were you. Take him camping with you down at the Valley for a while, and keep him away from people. Let things settle down in the village. That will give you time to think things over too.

Fraser can come down and see if you need anything a few times a week and I am sure your friends will stop by for some adventure. Be careful with that gun of yours if you plan to take it."

"Ok Dad, thanks. That's what I'll do," I said, my anger starting to cool.

The following day I packed my tent and gear. It took two trips to get everything I needed for a couple of weeks and on my second trip I took Jerry with me down to Three Cliffs Woods. We could hang out there for a while, and there was plenty of space and things to do in the Valley for both Jerry and me. I had also brought my 4/10 cartridge gun and fishing gear so that I could hunt and fish.

As we walked across the golf links to the valley, I pondered over what my father had said. It was good advice and he meant well, wanting to save me from the heartbreak of having something happen to Jerry. Jerry was half tame and half wild, and therein was the problem. But could I not protect him, I pondered? I could when I was with him, but not when he was away on his own somewhere. A battle raged within my heart and mind, as to what I could do. I don't think anyone understands just how much Jerry means to me. He's the most wonderful friend I've ever had in my life! And I didn't want to imagine my life without him.

JERRY THE MAGPIE

I'll never forget that golden morning when I found you
having fallen out of your nest.
I picked you up and undid my jacket, and held you warm
against my breast.
Who is this precious life that I hold and
somehow know that
I need so much? And yet,
I do not know what the future holds
for us.
I was a boy, and you a young magpie!
How strange and unusual
people said that you and
I would walk a journey together instead.
How could it start, and where would it end,
they asked?
A boy and his magpie, riding a bike so fast!
A friendship began which grew into love,
far more wonderful
than the moon and stars above!
Only God could know where we'd go and
give me all your love.
And I am changed forever,
because of Jerry Magpies Love,
I love you Jerry!
And thank you God above!

I set up our tent just inside the woods, so we could look out across the valley, and see how high the tide was by looking at the river. We only had a short walk down to Three Cliffs Point and around to Pobbles Bay, Jerry's and my most favourite place!

Jerry sat upon my shoulders and pecked my ears almost the whole time I was setting up our tent. And it was as if he knew that we needed to stay close together. It reminded me of the way things were before he learned to fly. Or was he sensing my insecurity about the future and my needing him close? "We are on a new adventure," I told him. "We have to stay away from the village for a while, and not steal anyone's earrings, Old Boy! Does that ring a bell? And I would have loved to have seen you landing on that woman's perm, when she had just got out of the hairdressers!" We both chuckled.

Fraser, Bryce and Eli arrived in the valley in the late afternoon. I could see them from our lookout just outside the tent, and I waved them over.

"We heard from Fraser about Die Book and Pencil, Kings," Bryce said, "and him wanting to put Jerry in the bird gardens. We won't let it happen Kings! Don't worry."

"Damn right, we won't," I echoed, sounding proud and rebellious, "and if I have to live in the wild all summer with him, I will!"

The first week that Jerry and I camped in the valley, Fraser, Bryce and Eli came and spent time with us every day. We went fishing for trout in the Three Cliffs River, and cooked them on an open fire at the edge of the woods. We also caught some nice bass in the sea off Three Cliffs

Point. Every morning I fed Jerry on the little crabs that lived in the mud of the river, and in the evenings I took him around the point or over the cliff top depending on the tide, to Pobbles Cove, where he fed on his favourite food of all, Sand Hoppers! It was surely a nice break from digging worms at home, but as I watched Jerry foraging in the riverbed for crabs and rummaging in the grass for worms and grubs, I realized he was becoming more and more independent every day.

Just before dark, I hunted rabbits with my 4/10. Jerry didn't like the crackle of my gun. He would fly off for several minutes each time I fired it, and then return. He soon learned that the firing of the gun meant food, and got used to the noise. It was all worth the effort, we both agreed, as we cooked the rabbits for our evening meals.

"You really could live in the wild, Kings!" Bryce and Eli exclaimed one evening as we sat around the fire and reminisced of our day.

"Yeah, I could, couldn't I," I acknowledged proudly. "Just think of it, no more living in the constraints of a house, washing dishes and tidying up, or listening to mothers or sisters complaining about having to clean up."

"You would know alot about that, Kings," my brother said. "I've never seen you wash a dish," and we all roared with laughter, including Jerry who almost fell off his perch in a nearby tree.

"Yeah, no more pissing around in houses for Jerry and I, lads. It's the outdoors from now on. We will stay here until the first day back at school if we have to. Won't we Old Boy!" Jerry made his 'magpie cackle', which was becoming more and more famous to us boys every day, and he flew up and down in agreement to what I'd said.

Bryce informed me that Olivia was missing me and wondering where I was. Fraser also said that Lorna Griffiths had phoned the house asking for me. Life is good, I pondered as I put another piece of wood on the fire, and we all sat in the loud listening silence of the valley, while the fire spat and crackled, and left each of us to dream our secret dreams underneath a crescent moon. We watched as the night clouds marched across the sky and drew their curtains covering the moon. Goodbye Mr. Moon, nice of you to come and visit, please come again soon.

On Thursday morning, Eli arrived in the valley late. Bryce and Fraser and I had already caught some trout, and were cooking them for breakfast. "Look what I've got," Eli said, holding a Herring Gulls egg in his hand. "The gulls have started laying their eggs on Pennard Cliffs."

This was big news for us all! We were all keen collectors of bird eggs in the spring and early summer months, depending on what species we were collecting. For example, Ravens nest and lay their eggs as early as February. I once found a nest with eggs as early as mid January. The Gulls tend to lay later in the year, usually in May and early June, and sometimes when the weather is more warm, in July.

"Don't worry Jerry," we all said. "We won't take your eggs if you build a nest and want to raise a family!" Fraser and I then looked at one another, as we thought of the nest and treasure we had found. "Don't say anything," I said quietly, and he nodded in agreement having read my lips.

Once the egg collecting was over, we traded eggs to add to our collections, just like we did with the football

cards. Collecting bird eggs was not popular with many people,and it was illegal to collect certain species, such as owls
and hawks, and other birds of prey. But we had lots of fun
doing it, and often made daring climbs high up in trees for
buzzard and sparrowhawk eggs, or climbed along ledges
high up on Pennard Cliffs for fulmor or guillemot eggs.
'Crazy!' My father called it. But he had the best collection
of all. And we often made extra pocket money by selling
him some of the rarer eggs. 'Stop encouraging the boys to
collect bird eggs', my mother would say to my father after
we had made our latest deal. But Dad was one of the boys
when it came to collecting bird eggs. He would just say,
don't let the police catch you with those eggs, or you're
liable to get yoked! If they do catch you, you're on your
own, and don't involve me! 'We won't Dad', I always said,
as we traded him a rare egg.

Fraser and I were fortunate to have a Dad who could
be like one of the boys when he wanted to. He knew where
to draw the line too, from being a friend and then being
able to switch over to being a father, and Fraser and I had
grown to respect that, as well as our friends who often said
they wished they had a dad like ours. I think it helped to
drive my mother mad, knowing that her husband was half
man and half boy at the same time! Be thankful he's not a
werewolf, Mum, and leave Dad alone!

After seeing Eli's Herring Gull egg, it was a unani-
mous decision that egg collecting season had begun, and we
all arranged to meet at 9:00 am at Pennard Stores tomorrow morning.

Jerry and I had a good night sleep in the tent, and
were first to arrive at the store in the morning. "Don't you
bring your magpie in the store, Kingsley," Mrs. Ridgley
said as she opened up the store.

"Don't worry, I won't. He's home in the aviary," I said lying through my teeth while feeling his warm body safely hidden in my jacket. "I'm just waiting for my brother and my friends."

"See that you don't ever bring him in this store again!" she said angrily.

"It doesn't take much brains to understand why she's so angry, does it Old Boy," I whispered, tilting my head towards Jerry. "You stole the meat right off the counter the other day, didn't you? And you scared the customers. It's ok Jerry Old Boy. You can still be Long John Jerry! But we have to behave for a while, and keep lying low, you know what I mean? Oh, don't look at me that way, Old Boy! Everything is cool alright. And as soon as the others arrive, I will send Bryce into the store to buy some Cornish pasties, and I will split one with you ok? It will be a nice change from fish and rabbit won't it."

Just then the boys arrived on their bikes. "Hey Kings, great to see you! How was your night in the tent? Where's Jerry?"

I pointed silently at the lump inside my jacket and replied, "It was just the way we like it. The boys chained up their bikes to a lamppost and started heading into the store for some refreshers and pop. "Hey, wait a moment!" I gestured waving my hands. "Jerry and I are barred from going into the store now. Can you get us 10 refreshers and a Cornish pasty, Bryce? Here's 60 pence."

"Sure thing, Kings! Why are you guys barred anyway?"

"Jerry nicked some roast beef right off the counter a few weeks ago."

Bryce laughed, and said, "good on you Jerry Boy," and then went into the store.

The boys seemed to be taking forever in the store, and Jerry and I were biting at the bit for a Cornish pasty! Finally they came out with the refreshers and our pasties and we walked around the corner onto West Cliff Road. Jerry and I had half a pasty each, and I put the other one away in my backpack for lunch. We all sat on a stone wall, chewing our refreshers and making plans as to which part of the cliffs we would start looking for eggs. Jerry looked stuffed! After downing half a cornish pasty, he just sat there as content as a magpies version of a couch potato. "Are you full, Old Boy?" I asked, although it was obvious he was. He just waddled about between us collecting the wrappers from our refreshers, and then just stood over them for the longest time. Usually he would fly from shoulder to shoulder until he had visited us all.

Just then an angry looking woman came around the corner and saw Jerry.

"Shit, we're busted," I said to the boys as she came up to us and demanded to know who Jerry belonged to!

"He's mine," I announced proudly!

The woman looked me up and down, and said, "he should be put away in a zoo! Or better still, destroyed!"

"I'll tell you something, you fat cow," I replied. "If I had a face like yours I'd teach my arse to talk!" The old bat huffed and puffed and if she was a wolf she would have blown our house down as she trudged back around the corner.

Fraser and Eli roared with laughter, but Bryce said, "oh shit! That was my neighbour, and she's sure to tell my mother."

"Well she had it coming!" I replied, still angry. "How dare she talk about Jerry like that. I guess I shouldn't have brought Jerry back to the village so soon after his crimes," I said to Bryce. "And don't worry," I assured him. "If she says anything to your folks, I'll take full blame for what I said." Unfortunately, Bryce's neighbor was the same woman with the perm that Jerry had landed on, and then stole her earring.

"Come on boys," I said. "Let's get out of here and over to the cliffs before any more trouble comes along. See Jerry, Grandma was right when she said, your sins will find you out!" Eli continued to laugh, and I don't think he'd stopped since I called the woman names.

We decided to start egging along the cliffs above Foxhole Bay. Foxhole Bay has a rugged cliff formation, with ledges and outshoots of rocky crags and grassy knolls, that the seabirds built their nest on. There are even some ancient bone caves, like Minchin Hole, Bosco's Den, and Bowen's Parlour, to name a few, that are hidden high in the rocks where you can find rock dove nests, high on the ledges inside the caves. Sometimes, though rare, you can find a rock pipit nest. Eli and I had found one last year, and got a rock pipit's egg each, and not up for trades!

Bryce is the best climber of all of us, or the 'maddest of the mad' as my father called it. I called our climbs gutsy and brave. Any way you look at it, Bryce is an amazing climber, and he has been rewarded by his courage and skill, in having one of the best egg collections on the whole Gower Peninsula. I came in second as far as being brave was concerned, but when I got scared, I got the shakes real bad, which makes it doubly dangerous when I was climbing along a thin ledge a hundred or more feet above the sharp limestone rocks and crashing waves below. Many people have fallen to their deaths from Pennard Cliffs, and we were crazy enough to risk our lives for a bird's egg. If any of our folks really knew the risks we took on the cliffs, they would have jumped out of their skins!

One time I climbed down a sheer cliff face to a Raven's nest near Hunts Bay. The nest itself was about 60 feet down from the cliff top, and about 90 feet up from the crashing waves and sharp rocks below. Bryce wasn't with us on this occasion, but Fraser and Eli were. I managed to reach the nest alright, which was as large as my Dad's motorcycle! The Ravens had been nesting there for over 70 years according to local bird watchers, building upon the nest and making repairs from year to year. They are very much like a magpie's nest, only ravens nests don't have roofs, unless they build under an overhanging rock cover, which many of them do. But this nest was exposed to the sea winds like no other I'd seen.

When I arrived at the nest, the raven that had been sitting on its eggs, took to the air and started to dive bomb me! Its mate soon arrived and joined in the attack and I got the shakes. All I could do was sit in the nest like some overgrown chick, and cover my eyes! Fraser shouted, "shit Kings! Hang on! What do you want us to do?"

"Go and get Bryce," I shouted, "and bring a rope!" Fraser stayed at the top of the cliff and tried to calm me down, while Eli raced to Bryce's house to get help.

"Just keep calm," Fraser shouted, "and try not to move!" I stopped waving my arms to fend off the ravens who continued with their dive bombing, and one's feet pulled through my hair as it almost landed on me! I moved now, shifting my body in the nest, and several twigs and small branches fell to the depths below, and I shook like a leaf.

"Fraser is right," I said to myself. "I must keep still or this whole nest is going to pull away from the rocks! Please God help me to calm down, and stop them dive bombing me, so that I don't fall!"

Fortunately Bryce was home, and after what seemed like an eternity, he and Eli arrived with a rope. Bryce threw the rope down to me and I was able to catch it. "Hold on with both hands!" he shouted. I wasn't going to argue! The three boys heaved on the rope, and slowly but surely up I came with the ravens in pursuit.

"Shit boys! That was close, you saved my life for sure!"

Back to today.

We started our adventure by climbing down from the cliff top and picking up a sheep path heading eastward towards Minchin Hole bone cave. "I want to find a rock pipits nest," Bryce said, as we walked in single file along the narrow path, and I tried not to look down at the sharp rocks that snarled out of the sea like a monster's teeth waiting for one of us to fall.

"It's around the next bend," I said, remembering the terrain from when I walked this precarious path less than three months ago. The four of us stood silent as we stood at the entrance of Minchin Hole.

Minchin Hole as previously mentioned, is one of the ancient bone caves of Pennard Cliffs, and the feeling at the entrance, is one of a haunting timelessness. One can easily imagine going inside and meeting a cave clan, or a wild animal from caveman days. Old red Sandstone with smooth Limestone rocks sunken and patterned into the dry clay, welcomes you like a caveman's carpet ushering you into the strangest of rooms. There is a strong almost unpleasant smell of seabird excrement in and around the entrance, which I'm sure wasn't there when the caveman that dwelt here ruled his roost.

I imagined the Cave woman who lived here being a clean creature, and wrapped in her animal skin firs and leather hide shoes, kept a clean home for her clan. Eli said, with the imagination of an extinct rhinoceros, "maybe she smelt like George Matthews."

Once through the entrance, the still heavy air and the high cathedral ceiling grip your senses like few other places do, and both Bryce and I thought we felt a ghost. I would go as far as saying that this experience upon the senses is unique to caves. There is a feeling of nakedness and barrenness within these walls, that calls out quietly, and when it knows that you are listening, it shouts out loud! An awakening of the human soul has occurred that walks like a haunting spirit between the unconscious to the con-sciousness almost immediately, and one is left standing, having been woken to an awareness that shouts out from your own soul and reaches back and converses with the beginning of time.

You can leave the cave, but it must be dealt with! You can't just pretend and deny that you feel something, heard something, saw something! It's real and you know it! Your soul talks back to it, and you don't have to under-stand it. You just know and acknowledge it. And that is what I did today, I spoke to the cave at its entrance, while Fraser, Bryce and Eli ran inside and climbed up its stone ledges at the back of the cave where Rock Doves nested, and sometimes rare seabirds like Fulmers, laid their eggs.

"I've found a Great Black Backed Gulls nest!" Fraser shouted. "It's got four eggs!"

"There's a Rock Doves nest with four eggs over here!" Eli shouted.

"And I've found a nest of something!" Bryce shouted after a long silence. "There are four eggs too, and they are blue with brown markings, but I don't know what they are."

"And I've found a cavewoman wrapped in a fur blanket, and she's naked!" I shouted. And laughter echoed back from the depths of the cave.

Jerry remained quiet on my shoulders, he seemed to know what I was experiencing in this timeless place. Or maybe he was experiencing it himself too. And that is the beauty of exploring the caves on Pennard Cliffs. There is always the surprise, and the treasures of awareness, and one's reaction to things both seen and unseen.

"Let's bring out the eggs and see what we've got," Bryce said, and we all sat outside the seagull shitting entrance with our spoils.

"Let the trading begin," Fraser announced.

"I've got three Rock Dove eggs," Eli said. "I left one in the nest so they can lay more and still bring up a clutch of chicks, and I'm keeping two for myself and trading one."

"I've got three Blacked Back Gull eggs," Fraser said, "and I also left one in the nest for those poor buggers. I'm keeping one and trading the others." It was Bryce's turn to announce his spoil.

"Look at these," he said, laying down three sky blue eggs with beautiful brown blotches on them. He had our undivided attention. They were rare and beautiful looking eggs that none of us had seen before.

"Look how oblong they are on one end," I commented. "I haven't seen any like that in the bird book." Even Jerry seemed interested and flew down from my shoulders. "No, you mustn't touch them, Old Boy," I said, "unless you lay some yourself. Now get back on my shoulders," and I lifted him up.

So we all wanted one of Bryce's eggs, but there were only three as he'd also left one in the nest to encourage the parent birds to lay more. This was something we all tried to do, and it most often worked. Many times we have returned to nests after leaving one or two eggs, and the parent birds have laid more. If all the eggs are taken, then it is more likely that the nest will be abandoned. It has often been said that birds can only count up to three. Who said it I don't know, and what that has got to do with this present conundrum is your guess as well as mine, dear reader.

Back to the story.

As I was saying, there were three eggs and four of us, not including Jerry of course. What did I have to trade? I thought. I think money will have to come into this equation, if I wanted to have one of those beautiful eggs, and then there was the added equation of my Dad, or was it a multiplication consideration? Dad would reward dearly for one of these beauties for his collection! Fraser and I looked at one another, doing the same math, but we kept quiet. Jerry took part in the deep contemplating silence that now filled the air outside the entrance of Minchin Hole, and I wondered if the cave family were looking on. Surely they rode upon the gentle breath of seabreeze that stirred in contemplation around us.

What should I offer? I heard the cogs of everyone's brain asking. Jerry then flew down again from my shoulders and turned his head from side to side, as if to say, 'Come on you numb skulls, let's make a decision here shall we?'

Bryce broke the silence, and said, "I'm selling one to your Dad, Kings." There goes me making a profit on Dad, I thought, and Fraser nodded at me obviously realizing the same thing. "So that leaves two," Bryce said, and I wondered why he wasn't keeping one for himself. Maybe he would come back later and take the last egg. No, not Bryce, but Eli might.

"I will give you two Rock Dove eggs and three pounds for one of the eggs," Eli said.

"Hmmm," Bryce contemplated. "Any other offers?" he asked. I wasn't the only one who had money for currency, I thought.

Fraser then made his offer and said, "I'll give you two Black Backed Gull eggs and two pounds."

Bryce pondered the offer for a few moments, and then said, "what about you Kings?"

"Three quid and one of my best football cards," I answered.

"Which one?" he asked.

"Peter Boneti, the Chelsea goalie."

"I'll take the Black Backed Gull eggs, and the two pounds, Fraser," Bryce said, and the first deal was done. Eli then offered me one of his Rock Dove eggs and two pounds for Peter Boneti.

"It's a deal," I said, and we shook hands.

We decided to continue our trading at my place, as Eli wanted his football card today, and Bryce wanted to trade his special egg to my father. "I'm going to blow my egg when I get home," Fraser said, "and put it right in my collection."

Blowing eggs can be a precarious practice at the best of times, and over the years we have all cracked or completely shattered eggs while blowing them. It was as Dad said, a real art. To blow an egg you make two holes in the eggshell, one at each end. The end of the egg where you are applying pressure with your mouth, you only need to make a small pin hole, as you just want a small steady amount of pressure against the shell. At the other end where the yoke will be exiting the shell, you make a larger hole so that the yoke can flow more easily out. Not too large a hole though, as the bigger the hole in the egg, the less its value, and it looks awful too. You start by blowing gently and building up the pressure until all the yoke shoots out of the other end. Last time Eli and I were blowing eggs at his place, his sister Debbie said we looked like hamsters having sex, and Eli laughed so much he burst his frickin' egg.

It is best to hold the egg very gently with both your hands using both thumbs and forefingers gently engulfing the egg. If you blow too hard, or put too hard a grip on the shell, the egg will explode! Very costly if it is a rare egg that you have found, and risked life and limb to get it. Dad had Fraser and I practice on chicken eggs, much to my mothers disapproval. I think the river of yoke across the kitchen floor didn't help matters in the least, and Fraser and I came away with egg on our faces, so to speak, or should I say cluck.

Back to the present.

Dad seemed quite amused as we arrived at the house like a fleet of trading ships, he called us, and it was straight down to business. "And get Jerry out of the house, Kings, before your mother sees him. He's rather a sore topic around here these days. So what do you boys have to offer?" Dad said, rubbing his hands together like Captain Blyth.

"I've got a Black Backed Gulls egg for you Dad!" Fraser said, full of enthusiasm.

"I've already got one," he said, "but I like the blotches of black and grey on this one! How much?"

"Two pounds," Fraser replied.

"Two pounds, that's daylight robbery!" Dad said with a smile, and we all laughed. Then he handed my brother the two quid. "Alright, alright, next offer," he said, rubbing his hands and blowing on them like an impatient pirate. Dad was a hero in my friends eyes, a grown man, but just like one of the boys who they could wheel and deal with, and they all liked him alot.

"Look, Mr. Hill," Bryce said. "Look at this beautiful blue egg with brown blotches, and it's more oblong in shape than any of the others. I don't know what species it's from."

"Let me take a closer look," Dad replied, and he picked it up to inspect it. "What a beautiful egg!" He exclaimed, and he left the room to get his book on British Birds Eggs. We all looked at Bryce with envy. If he played his eggs right, he could make a "fiver" on this deal! Dad returned to the room with the book already open. "By jove look at this!" he said, pointing to one of the eggs in the book, and we all crowded round to see.

"It's a Guillemot, I believe! It is very similar in size and shape to the Razorbill and Black Guillemots eggs. But you can see how the egg is more oblong and thin on the one side, just like in the book." As we looked at the Guillemot eggs in the book, we could see that there were at least four variations in their colours, ranging from off-white with brown blotches, to brown base with cream blotches, and a very dull brown with darker brown, and almost black markings. "I like the blue with the brown blotches, like this one!" he said, holding Bryce's egg in his hand. "Well Bryce, Guillemots are quite rare around here, you usually have to go to the Rhossili Ledges to find one. I'll give you a fiver for it."

"It's a deal, Mr. Hill. Thank you very much!" Bryce said as proud as punch. Wow! Bryce just made more money than Fraser and I had found in the magpie's nest. Five quid! Bryce was the big winner today!

Chapter Fifteen

Black Morris

After our wheeling and dealing with Dad, Eli headed home, and Fraser went up to the bedroom to blow his eggs. He'd done pretty good too, having made a trade for one of the Gull eggs.

I got Jerry from the aviary and headed back with Bryce to his house, as I wanted to see Olivia. When we arrived at Bryce's, Jerry and I were greeted with hostility. Black Morris answered the door, and said that Olivia was not allowed to see me anymore, and could I leave the property immediately.

Bryce apologized for his words and went into the house. Meanwhile as soon as Black Morris had closed the door, Olivia called out from her bedroom window with just above a whisper. "Kingsley, meet me at the castle in an hour," and she closed the window.

What shall I do? I pondered, feeling pain in my heart. I wanted to go back and bang on the door! I didn't trust Black Morris as far as I could throw him. And I especially didn't trust him around Olivia. I had always had this uneasy feeling that he was doing something to Olivia. I knew for a fact that he beat his wife, and I had been a witness to that atrocity! Shall I go and kick the door down and make sure he isn't hurting Olivia? I pondered. No, I'll see if she meets me at the castle first. And if she doesn't, I'll know that something is wrong, and I'll go back to make sure she is ok. "What do you think, Jerry Old Boy?" He nibbled my ear and said, let's head over to the castle.

We arrived at the castle and waited for Olivia to arrive. Jerry amused himself by flying up and down from the castle walls, and I chewed on a stalk of grass and wondered what had made Black Morris so hostile today. Not that he was anything other than cold and indifferent towards me at any time. Was it because of what I said to his neighbour I wondered? She probably told him that I called her a fat cow, and the other names.

"What do you think, Old Boy?"

"Oh, you were just being protective over me, Kings."

"Thanks Old boy! I certainly am protective over you, but I shouldn't have called her those names. Now Olivia is not allowed to see me.

We waited for what seemed like a long time, and then suddenly, Jerry flew off the castle wall and headed out across the golf course. "What do you see?" I called out after him, and I climbed up the castle wall to take a look.

There in the distance was Olivia, and Jerry had flown all the way to meet her. I climbed back down from the wall and waited for them to arrive.

"Hi handsome man," Olivia said. "Fancy meeting you here." She was in good spirits. I was half expecting her to be upset, knowing she wasn't allowed to see me.

"Fancy seeing you here," I replied with a smile. "It's so good to see you," and I hugged her tightly!

"Oh Kings! I'm sorry, I'm so embarrassed!"

"No, I'm sorry," I said. "I shouldn't have called your neighbour names like that."

"Well, according to Bryce, she had it coming, Kings! Saying such nasty things about Jerry and wanting to get rid of him. The truth is, my Dad just needed an excuse to stop me from seeing you, because he doesn't like you, or anyone else for that matter, who shows me any attention. He feels threatened and jealous of you, because he knows how much I love you!" Now I could see that Olivia was upset and wrestling with her emotions inside. And I pondered quietly to myself as to what I could say in this situation.

Finally I spoke and said, "there must be something very wrong with your father for being jealous of me, and anyone else who gives you any attention." I felt angry and wanted to say more about Black Morris! I decided to bite my tongue however, and to listen to what else Olivia said, before saying anything else.

"And what's more," Olivia went on to say, 'my Dad has beaten my Mum again, and given her another black eye." Now I couldn't hold my tongue any longer.

"You have to call the police, and have them take him out of the house. He can't go on abusing your Mum like this. And it's not the first time, I know! I saw your mum's eye the other day and the fear in her eyes. There are laws, you know, to protect battered women. And what if it were you, Olivia, or your brother that he was abusing, what then? What provokes him to be so violent? Do you know?" Olivia's eye's now filled up with tears, and I held her again in my arms. "You can tell me," I said. "It's alright."

"All I know is that my Mum accused him of touching me, and he went crazy and punched my mother!" Olivia now cried uncontrollably, and pleaded with me not to talk anymore about it.

"Alright," I said, "but please tell me one more thing. I need to know that he is not touching you!" Olivia now clinged to me, and her whole body began to tremble, and in that moment she had already answered my question. I knew there was something very wrong with that man, I thought, I knew it! I felt it the first time I met him! I wanted to call the police! I needed to know that she would be safe when she went home, and wouldn't be punished for sneaking out and seeing me. I felt so helpless, and I spoke aloud to Olivia again. "I love you," I said, "and I want to protect you."

"Don't worry, my love," she said, trying to reassure me. "My Dad won't be home when I get back, he goes and stays at his mothers every time he has a fight with Mum. It's as regular as clockwork, he beats her up and then leaves. Can we just enjoy our time together Kings, and not talk about this, you're the only thing that's right in my life and I don't want anything to spoil our time together."

"Alright," I replied, and I kissed the tears from her face. She stopped shaking and smiled again.

"It was so great to have Jerry come and meet me," she said. "He can fly very well now."

"Yes, he can," I replied. "He has grown his long tail feathers now, and you should see him balance in the wind, when he's perched on a wire or a fence, or riding on the handlebars of my bike. I'm very proud of him."

"And protective," Olivia added, and we both laughed! "And I'm really glad you called our neighbor a cow. It is high time someone put her in her place. She is such a snob and doesn't have a nice word to say about anyone." We both laughed and it felt good to break the tension.

"What's that you are saying, Jerry?" We both asked, as he made his cackling magpie sound. "Laughter is the best medicine," he replied, and he cackled some more. It certainly is, we agreed.

It was a lovely evening as Olivia and I looked down from our hill overlooking the valley. Everything seemed peaceful and still, unlike the turmoil that was going on in Olivia's life and family, and in some ways, within our relationship, with her father forbidding her to see me, and me being away from home and living out in the wild with Jerry. Life's challenging events always seem to have a cause and effect, in bringing to the forefront our feelings and emotions in a passionate expression, at least they do for me. But I was learning that Olivia and her mother often hid their feelings inside, and wore masks of disguise to cover up what was really going on in their lives. Like when I saw Mrs. Morris with a blackeye for the first time. She said she had banged her face on a cupboard, but as I looked into her eyes, her soul shouted out to me, 'Kingsley, look at me, I'm being abused, and I'm in so much pain!'

Bryce is in complete denial about the whole thing. When I ask him how things are going at home, he clams up tighter than an oyster. I had to keep my conversations light and fun with Bryce, or he would soon make an exit from whatever we were doing.

My Grandmother said that nature can calm and soothe the human spirit, and reflect peace, just like it did for Olivia and I this evening. As we watched the sparkling waters of the Pennard Pill winding its way to the waiting arms of the open sea, we felt its waters stealing away our spirits to a place of wonderful peace. And I think that is one of the reasons God created the quiet flowing waters, was to still the anxious souls of the children of men.

THE PENNARD PILL

The Pennard Pill is at a hush,
as she flows slowly to the waiting arms of the leaping sea,
uttering only
a few silent words as she skips along the pebbles,
remembering the days when she was but
a young girl, wearing her summer dresses and
painted toes and dancing in the Spring.
She is ancient now, but her joyous fount, remains
sparkling and young,
as boys and girls come to play,
and swim and fish, in her enchanted waters.
And like
the pebbles she has rounded through
the passages of time,
I only need to stand in her waters,
to be reminded that
She is mine!
The Pennard Pill, a stream without time!

End of Part One

www.ingramcontent.com/pod-product-compliance
Lightning Source LLC
Chambersburg PA
CBHW070343200726
48294CB00003B/773